Robert Wells

Elvis:
The Siege of Graceland
and Other Stories

To Julie and Leonie,
my dearest friends,

Elvisly Yours

Rob Wells

novum ◢ pro

This book is also available as e-book.

www.novum-publishing.co.uk

© 2022 novum publishing

ISBN 978-3-99107-987-3
Editing: Nicola Grün
Cover photos: Amuzica,
Thomas Milewski | Dreamstime.com;
V-One Design Solutions
Cover design, layout & typesetting:
novum publishing
Internal illustrations: www.alamy.com

The images provided by the author
have been printed in the highest
possible quality.

www.novum-publishing.co.uk

Contents

1. The Siege of Graceland

"It's true that sequels are doing great business at the box office." Colonel Parker is on the phone to Hal Wallis, his great friend and producer of many of Elvis's movies. "I agree that maybe we should do a sequel to 'GI Blues'. The fans loved that film. Just a minute, Hal. Bubba is waving a piece of paper at me."

The Colonel tells his assistant if it is an invoice to put it in the pending tray, which, of course, as far as Bubba is concerned, is like saying 'abandon hope all ye who enter here'.

Resuming his conversation with Hal Wallis, the Colonel says, "Now let me get this straight. Your idea is that Elvis goes back to Germany. But this time he is a General and he's going to sort out the Russians and save Berlin. The working title will be Checkpoint Elvis. Yea, I like that. And can we get Juliet Prowse again who was in 'GI Blues'? You say you'll come back to me next week with a script. Hold on Hal, Bubba is jumping up and down and still waving that piece of paper. I'll call you back."

Colonel Parker sits back in his chair, wafts away the thick clouds of cheap cigar smoke, and invites Bubba to explain what is going on.

"Why, sir, it's this letter from the US army and I must admit that I am mighty puzzled. It says Elvis is on something they call the Reserve List and he must report in the next seven days to somewhere called Camp Benedict Arnold. It's in Tumbleweed, Mississippi."

The Colonel goes for the full bluster and declares, "This is outrageous! That boy has served his time with Uncle Sam. Two whole years and he came back a hero. This whole thing is a big mistake!"

"A hero, Colonel, sir? I really didn't know that," comments Bubba innocently.

"Yes, they pinned a medal on his chest."

"Would that be the Good Conduct Medal, sir? Because it is my belief that every soldier got one of those, providing they didn't shoot the commanding officer."

"Don't quibble, Bubba," says the Colonel. "This is all a terrible mistake. We're going to ignore this and it will go away. Trust me."

Elvis, the Colonel, Hal Wallis, and Steve Sholes, RCA's top record producer, are going through the script of the 'GI Blues' movie sequel. Hal describes how the General, played by Elvis, has gone over the Berlin Wall and into the Russian zone to rescue Juliet Prowse when he is confronted by a group of Russian soldiers. While the fight is going on, the soundtrack will play Elvis singing a specially commissioned song called 'Caught Reds Handed'.

Elvis grumbles about it being another album movie but Hal Wallis shakes his head and assures him there'll just be a couple of songs. He looks meaningfully at the Colonel and adds that the movie will be a thriller with just a little hint of comedy, more Cary Grant than Dean Martin and Jerry Lewis. "My script boys see this as a breakout role for Elvis," adds Hal Wallis, winking slyly at the Colonel.

There is a rapid knocking at the door and Bubba bursts in saying, "Colonel, sir, come quickly."

Colonel Parker is affronted and looks around the room as if he has been interrupted while addressing a large audience at the United Nations. He tells his assistant that he is in the middle of a very important meeting and to please put a 'Do Not Disturb' notice on the door on his way out.

"I'm really sorry, sir, but I do think you should come to the front door. Right now. They want to arrest Elvis."

Colonel Parker sets his straw trilby on his head, brushes the cigar ash from his Hawaiian shirt, and approaches the front door with the slowness and stateliness of an elderly hippopotamus with rheumatism. Standing there are four members of the military police. The guy at the front introduces himself as Captain Ludendorf and says he has a warrant for the arrest of Elvis Presley. The Colonel looks perplexed and strokes several of his chins as if he is being asked to explain the Theory of Relativity and doesn't know where to begin.

He blows cigar smoke towards the Captain. "Arrest! Has rock and roll suddenly become illegal? Arrest! Surely not for being the most famous man in the United States, if not the world. And surely not for being a medal-winning hero."

"No one is above the law, sir. Mr. Presley failed to report to Camp Benedict Arnold as ordered and we are here to take him there."

The Colonel asks to see the warrant, takes his time reading through it, and hands it back. "That is a load of baloney, Captain," he asserts.

"I must ask you to step aside, sir, and allow me to do my duty," is the reply.

"I am Colonel Thomas Parker of the Virginia Fencibles and I outrank you. I'm saying that warrant is not valid. I order you to go back and get it checked." Minnie Mae has appeared next to the Colonel and she has a very convincing argument – she is pointing Granpappy Hood's old buffalo gun at Captain Ludendorf. "Elvis ain't leavin' the building, son", she declares. "You should be a-wearin' clown shoes an' a big red nose cus ah ain't never heard sich damn fool nonsense. You and yer boys need ter scoot reeeal fast cus mah trigger finger is a-startin' ter twitch."

At that moment they are joined by Elvis who leaps into his karate kill stance, makes a few chopping motions with his hands, and tells them, "You'll never take me alive." The Captain and his men retreat a few feet, while Elvis goes back into the house, roaring with laughter, saying, "I bet that scared them."

"Colonel, Ma'am, we will be back," replies Captain Ludendorf a little less confidently. "And next time Mr. Presley will be coming with us."

And that is how the siege of Graceland began.

A little while later, Elvis's grandmother, Minnie Mae, is sitting in a chair outside the front door with the buffalo gun resting across her lap. She is joined by her daughter, Aunt Delta, who is pulling a suitcase on wheels. "Thought ah'd join yer, Ma," she says.

"Planning ter stay the night," observes Minnie Mae, nodding towards the suitcase.

"Mebbe," answers Aunt Delta, who unzips it, to reveal that it is fitted out as a small cocktail cabinet complete with bottles, glasses, shaker, and ice bucket. "Can I fix yer a drink, Ma?"

"Sure thing, why not."

Inside the house, Priscilla, Elvis's wife, is fretful about Minnie Mae being outside. She pleads with Elvis: Is she going to be out there all night? What if she falls asleep? What if they rush the house? Shouldn't some of the boys be out there with her?

"Dodger is like a rattlesnake," he replies. "Her eyes might be closed, but behind those eyelids of hers, she's wide awake and ready to strike. With that old gun, she can hit a rat's eye at 200 paces and blow a hole in a tank with the same shot."

Colonel Parker adds that they cannot risk Elvis being outside in case the military police send in a snatch squad that somehow gets through. He tells them he needs to go and make some phone calls to the main TV channels and newspapers. "That fool of a military police captain has handed me a million dollars' worth of publicity."

He holds his hand out, palm upwards and tells them, "It feels like rain. I'm telling you, once the Colonel has finished, it's going to be raining dollars here at Graceland, heh heh heh."

Captain Ludendorf soon returns with double the number of military policemen and they are crouched behind their jeep that's parked halfway down the drive. One of the MPs who is training his binoculars on Graceland tells him, "Sir, I've got a clear shot. I can take out the old lady with the gun."

"Are you mad?" shouts the Captain, flinging his cap to the ground in anger. "Shoot Elvis's grandmother? We'd get lynched — and that's just what the army will do to us. Can you imagine if Elvis's fans were to get hold of us?"

"Sorry about that, sir. I thought we'd be covered by military necessity."

"Give me those binoculars, I think there's something going on." He focuses them on the front door, shakes his head, wipes the lenses clean, refocuses the binoculars, and mutters, "Oh no no no no. I don't believe this. What's he doing there? And how did he get in?"

Liberace walks out onto the portico of Graceland in a full-length white ermine coat draped over his shoulders, which Brother George carefully removes to reveal that Liberace is wearing a black diamante encrusted, long-tailed jacket with a piano keyboard pattern on both lapels, matching black shorts and knee-length white socks. Brother George returns with an ornate gilt chair which he flicks with a monogrammed duster and puts it next to Minnie Mae so that Liberace can sit down. He returns again with a small antique side table on which he puts a fabulous Louis XlVth candelabrum, the finest in their collection.

"Good morning Minnie Mae and Aunt Delta," says Liberace.

"Mornin' Lee," replies Minnie Mae.

"As very dear friends of Elvis, Brother George and I wanted to be here to stand alongside him in his hour of peril. We didn't want to bring Momma in case things got, well, you know, a bit rough."

"Why thankee, Lee," Minnie Mae tells him. "There's no knowin' how things are gonna go. But y'all can bet yer best grand piano that they ain't a-takin' Elvis. He ain't a-going ter Viet Nam. An' he ain't gonna be fightin' them King Kong." "You mean the Viet Cong," says Liberace helpfully.

"Yea, an' them as well."

"Oh Lordy no," groans Captain Ludendorf as he continues to look through his binoculars at the front of Graceland. He did not think it could get any worse, but it just has. He watches as James Brown dances and does a couple of splits on his way across the length of the portico before ending with a spin on one leg in front of Minnie Mae and Liberace. "Hi brothers and sisters," he greets them. "Soul Brother Number One is here to join the cause and stand shoulder to shoulder with Elvis and Liberace."

Brother George brings him a chair and Aunt Delta offers to fix him a drink. And then adds, as a little joke, only if he says "Please Please Please."

An hour later there is a media frenzy, the flames of which have been fanned by Colonel Parker, outside the gates of Graceland. Captain Ludendorf is on his radio phone to request advice on what to do, and for more back-up. There is a cavalcade of TV outside broadcast units and newspaper cars stretching all the way back to downtown Memphis. Walter Cronkite, Dan Rather, and Walter Winchell are standing at the Music Gates with their camera crews doing live broadcasts.

Thanks to the information that has been passed on by the Colonel, Walter Cronkite is telling millions of TV viewers, "Is this what the United States of America has come to? I cannot believe it, and you, the viewers won't either. But I am witnessing with my own eyes a terrible injustice. Elvis Presley, the King of Rock and Roll, a man who served his country with honour and dignity, a man who was awarded a medal, is to be arrested for what I am assured is a trumped-up minor misdemeanour. This is America's Day of Shame."

Dan Rather is telling his viewers that Elvis's grandmother will link arms with Liberace, James Brown, and Hal Wallis to form a human shield to defy the military police. "I am reliably informed they will tell them: 'Shoot if you dare, but you're not taking Elvis'."

One of the TV channels has brought along a couple of retired generals to tell viewers just how they would bring a speedy and successful conclusion to the siege.

Captain Lundendorf is under orders to end the siege as quickly as possible because the army is being made to look like a bunch of fools on millions of TV screens and in millions of newspapers across the world. How can the mightiest military machine in history be seen to be failing to capture one man?

"If we can't do this, what chance have we got against the Russians?" a four-star general tells Captain Ludendorf from behind his desk at the Pentagon. "Get this mission accomplished now!"

"I think I need more reinforcements, sir," he replies. "We may come under fire. At least one of them guarding Elvis Presley is armed." (He neglects to add that it is a little old lady with an antique buffalo gun.)

Later, the Captain scans the portico of Graceland through his binoculars to see that only Liberace and James Brown are sitting there. This looks like it is the right moment to make his move. With a wave of his arm, two armoured personnel carriers and a platoon of military policemen on foot with bayonets fixed begin to trundle up the drive.

As they come to a stop outside Graceland, Charlie Hodge, Elvis's buddy and faithful gofer who has been with him since he served in the army in Germany, opens the front door. He is only 5 foot 3 inches tall and the Elvis Vegas jumpsuit he is wearing is so baggy that you could get another couple of Charlies inside. But he shouts out, "I am Elvis!" Next to emerge is Colonel Parker, bursting out of a Vegas jumpsuit and with his hair dyed black, to stand alongside Charlie and announce, "I am Elvis!" The next one to join them and proclaim defiantly "I am Elvis" is Dr. Nick. The procession of Elvises in Vegas outfits with their hair dyed black continues to walk out of the front door one after another and shout "I am Elvis!": Bubba, the Colonel's assistant; Red and Sonny West, cousins and members of the Memphis Mafia, who are in charge of security; Vernon, his father; Priscilla, his wife; grandmother Minnie Mae; Aunt Delta; his hairdresser Larry Geller; movie producer Hal Wallis; Brother George and record producer Steve Sholes. Even Lamar Fike, a long-time member of the Memphis Mafia, steps out on to the portico. Although, unlike the others, he is too fat to squeeze into a jumpsuit, he wears a tan-coloured linen suit, which has enough cloth to make a small circus tent, and a black wig and declares, "I am Elvis." The last to come out of Graceland is Old Shep, Elvis's dog, with a card around his next saying 'I am Elvis'. He flops down and starts scratching his fleas.

"Captain Ludendorf, sir, I can report we have 16 Elvises if you include the dog," reports a Sergeant. "They cannot all be the right Elvis, sir."

"No Sergeant, but one of them surely is. So let's leave the dog and take all the rest of them to Camp Benedict Arnold and we'll sort it out there."

"Very good, sir. And what about Liberace and James Brown? What should we do with them?"

"Well they are not Elvis are they, Sergeant? We'll leave them here. They can look after the dog."

And so the convoy, with 15 Elvises sitting on benches in an armoured personnel carrier, sets off for Fort Benedict Arnold, followed by the media caravan of TV outside broadcast trucks and cars and taxis carrying journalists and photographers.

Walter Cronkite is telling viewers, "I can assure you that I am not making this up. This is really happening here in Memphis. Elvis Presley must be the most famous and easily recognisable person in the world. But the military police here at the siege of Graceland have arrested and are taking away 15 people claiming to be Elvis because they didn't know which is the real one." The camera pans from Walter Cronkite to show 15 weird-looking Elvises sitting in the back of the personnel carrier. "Folks are saying that this could be the biggest military blunder since Napoleon set off for Moscow," Walter Cronkite continues.

The Captain decides that what they need – and quick – is an identity parade to end all the 'I am Elvis' nonsense. So he decides to send for George Klein, the Memphis disc jockey, to be brought to the army camp to pick out the real Elvis. He has been a close friend since they were at high school together, and if anyone knows who Elvis is, it's George. But as he walks along the line of 15 Elvises standing against the wall, he notes the sly wink from Colonel Parker. He walks back along the line, stopping to look carefully at each one in turn, and all the while fighting hard to stop himself from laughing. After a lot of rubbing his chin and shaking his head, he admits, "I don't know. They could all be Elvis."

Captain Ludendorf is incredulous. "'How on earth do you make that out? Some of them are women. At the very least how can they be Elvis?"

George shrugs his shoulders and tells him, "I haven't seen Elvis for a couple of months and, you know, people can change."

The Captain, who can hear sniggers from some of the Elvises in the line-up, could weep with frustration.

As a result of a tip-off, the terrible truth dawns on Captain Ludendorf and the military police: they have taken 15 Elvises into custody – in an event that is being broadcast and published across virtually every TV station and newspaper around the world – and not one of them is the real Elvis. In fact, the truth is that they have left him behind at Graceland, dressed as Liberace, the two of them having swapped outfits.

Captain Ludendorf is told he is wanted on the phone in his office and that it is urgent.

"Is that Private Ludendorf?" says a voice.

"No, this is Captain Ludendorf."

"No, I was right the first time Private. This is the Commander in Chief, President Nixon. I've been watching all this from the Oval Office. You have made the armed forces a laughing stock. Millions are watching and they have not laughed so much at the army since Sergeant Bilko was the top-rated show on TV. Even I couldn't stop myself laughing at times and I'm the Commander in Chief."

Earlier President Nixon and his team of advisors had to suspend work on a draft finance bill, as well as postpone a meeting with the Secretary General of the United Nations, in order to find a way out of the crisis developing over the arrest of Elvis. Or what has now transpired into a major military show of force to arrest the wrong Elvis. The wrinkles on the President's face deepen and beads of sweat pop out on his brow as he pours himself a drink of scotch. An aide hurries into the Oval Office to report that Buckingham Palace has been on the line; The Queen of England is worried about Mr. Presley and will the President call her as soon as possible. "How in hell can this have happened?" asks the President emptying his glass.

"It's a snafu, sir," says an aide.

"How the hell did Elvis's name come up anyway?" he asks and at a nod of his head, an aide refills his glass.

"Clearly, he wasn't on any Reserve List. What a farce. But luckily, it's nothing to do with me," he says to his aides. "I'm as clean as a whistle on this one. As for this idiot Ludendorf... haven't we got a weather station in the Artic Circle? I want him there on a five-year mission as soon as this thing is cleared up."

"One last thing, Mr. President," says an aide. "This could play very badly in the polls, I mean trying to arrest Elvis of all people – Mr. America himself. The voters might well see this as a monumental screw-up and we may have to do something big to be seen to be doing the right thing by Elvis. We've got to claw back credibility big time."

Eventually, President Nixon and his aides manage to concoct a story involving a mix-up with names that they hope will work and will take the heat off of the situation. Private Ludendorf is ordered to return to Graceland to apologise to Elvis, his family, and entourage and then to hold a press conference at the Music Gates.

"The army and the military police want to apologise for what was a clerical error," he tells the media. "We were acting on the information given to us but the person we should have actually detained was an Alvin Priestley and not Elvis Presley. Obviously, something must have gotten garbled in transmission. We are sorry but lessons have been learned and nothing like this will ever happen again. Meanwhile, the military police will ceaselessly continue to pursue and detain the said Alvin Priestley."

Elvis is in the Jungle Room watching a ball game and working his way through a giant bucket of popcorn when a phone call comes through from President Nixon in the Oval Office.

"Elvis, as Commander in Chief, I sincerely want to apologise for the monumental blunder that resulted in the military police arriving at your home to arrest you. There was a clerical error over the name but I have personally intervened to ensure that it can never happen again," he reads with as much sincerity as he can muster from the script prepared by an aide.

"Huh huh," replies Elvis, who continues to watch the game and toss the occasional piece of popcorn at the TV screen at a particularly clumsy play.

"In recognition of your immense contribution to the American Way of Life, I am promoting you to Honorary FBI Agent At Large (First Class) which comes with a special gold plated badge."

Now he has Elvis's full attention. "Excuse me, Mr. President, sir, I really do appreciate that, but does this mean I'll be getting a bigger gun to help me in my duties?"

Sweat immediately breaks out on President Nixon's brow and he looks around in panic at his aides because this is not in the script. He motions for one of them to get him a scotch, while another aide, quicker thinking than the others, leans forward to whisper in his ear. The President listens and nods his head.

"Yes Elvis, Smith & Wesson will be specially commissioned to produce a pair of handguns more powerful than anything else in their range. Hopefully, you'll be able to feature them in your new movie. As Commander in Chief, I have authorised the army to provide all the assistance that you and your producers need in terms of military personnel and equipment, both here in the United States and in Berlin. Of course, I'll be there for the premiere with my wife."

Elvis thanks him on behalf of Colonel Parker and Hal Wallis and explains that the movie will be a sequel to 'GI Blues'. Has he seen that movie?

There is a look of terror on President Nixon's face as he looks down and realises his script doesn't deal with the conversation taking such a turn as this. What does he say? He mops the sweat from his brow and takes a fortifying drink while an aide whispers in his ear.

He didn't quite catch what he was saying but there is no time to ask him to repeat it, so the President continues, "You won't believe this, Elvis, but it's my daughter Patricia's favourite movie. I can hear her now singing that cute song, 'But I Don't Have a Wooden Leg'…"

Ends

2. Greta Garbo's Movie Comeback

Colonel Parker is looking tired, harassed and you could grate cheese on the stubble on his sagging chins. There are letters and invoices strewn across the floor of his office at Graceland and the air is thick with cigar smoke – like a London smog but much more dangerous to health.

As he walks in, Elvis keeps waving his hand in front of his face to beat away the choking fumes but the Colonel assumes it is a greeting and he waves back in return. He invites him to take a seat and puts down the phone while brushing off the small mounds of grey ash that have collected on the front of his orange Hawaiian shirt, like the debris of a volcanic eruption.

Elvis has arrived for an update on his manager's latest 'Big Idea' to breathe new life into his movie career and to make the sort of money that would represent the national debt of some small states. Only Colonel Parker could come up with an idea so breathtaking in its audacity and scope – nothing less than to persuade Greta Garbo to come out of retirement to make a musical with Elvis.

When he first mentioned this to him, Elvis's initial response, which he hoped would convey his utter incredulity, was to respond with an "huh-huh". While not particularly au fait with her career, he believed she hadn't made a film for more than 30 years and had certainly never made a musical.

"Why, Colonel, sir? Why Greta Garbo? After all these years, why shouldn't we just leave her to rest in peace in her retirement? Why don't we get Ann-Margret back again? She can dance and sing, she's Swedish and probably young enough to be Greta Garbo's granddaughter."

"Please, son, don't use words like 'rest in peace' about Greta Garbo. She is a movie legend, worshipped like a goddess, and if we can get her back in front of the cameras in a film with you, it will amaze the world. It will be the biggest sensation in pictures since the talkies."

Elvis looks again at his manager and asks where his assistant, Bubba, is and shouldn't he be there helping him with the chaos of the paperwork. "You're looking like 10 miles of bad road, Colonel, sir, if you don't mind my saying."

He tells Elvis that at this moment his assistant is sitting in a police station in Manhattan, helping them with their inquiries. He shakes his head sorrowfully and admits it is all his fault because he will not give up on his idea of shooting for the stars and getting Elvis and Greta Garbo in a film together. He conjures up images of huge posters proclaiming 'Garbo Sings' alongside 'Elvis Sings' and he is convinced it will be the first billion-dollar movie in history. The silver screen will become gold-plated.

He called in a lot of favours simply to get hold of her phone number, but when he did get through, she dismissed the whole idea as being ridiculous.

"It's the motherlode and just too good to give up without a fight," he says, continuing to puff distractedly on his Walmart cigar.

He tells Elvis how he followed up by sending her a copy of the script based on her old movie 'Queen Christina' that had been drafted by movie producer Hal Wallis's team of writers. It came back with the word 'No' scrawled across the front, and a PS: 'Leave me alone'. A personal letter and a photo of Elvis over which he had gone through so much trouble to autograph were similarly ignored. In a last throw of the dice (and gambling is something at which the Colonel is notoriously unlucky) he decided to send his assistant Bubba to New York to try and catch her and plead with her on one of those rare occasions when she emerges from her apartment on 52nd East Street.

Not unreasonably, Bubba demands to know, "What does she look like, Colonel? I'm flying blind here. I mean, how can I be sure if it is Greta Garbo I'm talking to?"

"Well, she'll be smartly dressed, in her mid-Sixties and wearing dark glasses," the Colonel replies.

"But that describes about half a million women living in Manhattan," Bubba protests bitterly.

Inevitably, the police pick him up after complaints are made that a man has been pestering women in the street for a couple of days, asking if they are Greta Garbo and would they like to be in a movie.

Colonel Parker admits he is worried that he can't think of a way of getting Bubba out of gaol, and also about the possible reputational damage if his assistant happens to mention his links to Elvis and himself. It could turn ugly in the press.

"The whole thing sounds like it's some sort of routine from Rowan and Martin's Laugh-in," declares Elvis. "I'd be roaring my head off if it wasn't so serious."

"What was that you said, son?" says the Colonel, suddenly becoming animated.

"I was just saying it sounds like a comedy sketch from a TV show."

"I think you've just given me an idea." He says he'll call Hal Wallis, who is currently in New York talking to the money men about financing the new movie with Garbo, and to see if he can help to get Bubba released.

The movie producer explains to the police captain that his officers mistakenly arrested Colonel Parker's assistant during the filming of a Candid Camera sequence for Elvis's next movie. Has he ever seen Candid Camera on TV? There is a shake of the head in reply. The idea is that there's a hidden camera that films how ordinary members of the public react differently in the same situation. It's just a bit of fun and it is a routine that's familiar to and popular with millions of Americans, apart from the police in Manhattan, that is, he adds. The bungling intervention of his two cops in arresting the Colonel's assistant has scuppered the whole project, he says, nodding his head sorrowfully.

"What can I say?" confesses the police chief.

"You can try sorry," replies Hal.

"To think, Elvis and my company, Paramount Pictures, were coming to New York to make his next big bucks movie and this is how we are treated," he continues, reaching for an imaginary trowel to lay it on as thickly as possible.

"I'm sure no one will want to blame you personally, Captain – May I just make a note of your name – but what would it have been worth to the Borough of Manhattan to have a film like this shot here? Who knows how Elvis is going to feel after all this... Who knows how far up the chain he will send this – the Police Commissioner, the Mayor, the State Governor, Frank Sinatra..."

By now the police chief is wringing his hands and saying he will go immediately to release Bubba and personally apologise to him.

"Let's hustle," says Hal. "We still may be able to save the movie."

When Bubba calls Colonel Parker on his release from the cells, he is told to go back to where Greta Garbo lives and try and persuade her – whatever it takes – to make the movie.

"But you cannot be serious, sir. In all probability, I'll be arrested again as a repeat offender. They'll throw the book at me and I'll end up in Rikers Island gaol."

But the Colonel is adamant and so Bubba gloomily heads back to 52nd East Street while pondering his possible fate as an inmate, sharing a cell with a tattooed thug serving life for murder. After hanging around for some hours and trying not to look furtive, he manages to sneak into the building behind the mailman as he presses the entry code buttons. Since knocking on the door of Garbo's apartment elicits no response, he gets down on his hands and knees and shouts through the letterbox near the bottom of the door, "I'm Bubba and I'm here on behalf of Colonel Thomas Parker and we want to talk to you about doing a movie with Elvis Presley."

"Blubber? Blubber?" he hears a woman muttering. "Why would anyone be called Blubber unless they are a whale?"

He bends down again to get his face as close as possible to the letterbox to say that his name is actually Bubba and they want her to star in a musical remake of one of her old films. He reels backwards when he suddenly sees a large pair of black sunglasses confronting him from the other side of the letterbox.

"I don't do musicals. I was a serious actress and now I am retired."

Remembering the Colonel's instruction about whatever it takes, there is one more thing he can try, so he tells her that he is going to slide a blank cheque through the letterbox and he wants her to fill it in with a number that has a lot of noughts. And that will be her fee for making the film.

There is a long silence and then the door of the apartment begins to open slowly.

"Do come in Mr. Blubber," she says and he enters a huge pine-panelled room with big windows and spectacular views of the East River. The Colonel said that although it was a long time ago, Greta Garbo was once the queen of Hollywood and that she is still revered; certainly, her apartment is a palace and she looks regal as she sits poised on a sofa as if waiting to have her picture taken for Vogue. He glances at a painting on the wall signed by someone called Renoir that looks a bit rough and ready in contrast with the cool elegance of the rest of the room. Perhaps a nice pale pine frame might help it blend in better with the rest of the décor.

She explains that she has been out of the movies for many years and would be grateful if he would help her with advice. "I'm very naïve how things are done nowadays but," she smiles as she wags her finger at him, "not so much that I won't notice if some noughts begin to disappear from that cheque you gave me. Is Jefferson Davis a new bank? I've not heard of it."

Bubba decides that caution is the best course and, rather than give some blanket assurances about integrity and honesty, he confines himself to saying that Hal Wallis and Colonel Parker are very experienced businessmen who have made many very successful movies together.

"Like 'Casablanca'," he adds and receives an approving nod of the head from Miss Garbo.

Seeking to quickly change the subject, he comments on the remarkable similarity of Elvis to the former movie actor John

Gilbert, not letting on, of course, that he was believed to be Greta Garbo's lover. It is a carefully planned throwaway line that he hopes might help clinch the deal.

"Hmm, I'm intrigued. Tell me more about this Elvis and the new film."

Colonel Parker touches heaven and hell within the space of a five-minute phone call with his assistant. He roars with delight, like a stag that has seen a mate on the other side of the glen, at the news that she wants to do the movie. But next, he is roaring like an enraged gorilla that has just missed out on a bunch of bananas at the news that Miss Garbo has asked Bubba to be her advisor. "You worm, you traitor," he yells down the phone. "You're supposed to be working for me and Elvis!"

"That's what I'm doing, Colonel, sir. And I clearly recollect you telling me to do whatever it takes."

He decides not to mention at this stage how many noughts Miss Garbo has put on the cheque.

Several days later Elvis, considerably cheered by the news that Greta Garbo has agreed to do the movie, is walking with a spring in his step down the corridor towards Colonel Parker's office to talk with him about setting up a meeting with his new co-star. As he goes to open the door, he hears Bubba declare with some emotion, "But sir, you can't do that! I'm sure the best years are still to come."

"I'm a businessman and sometimes you have to make tough decisions," retorts the Colonel heatedly.

Elvis knocks on the door and immediately senses the tension; he asks what is going on. "Surely, you can't be arguing about Miss Garbo?!" he demands. "That's what this meeting is all about, isn't it?"

"I wish it was, Elvis, but what is happening is that the Colonel is planning to get rid of his dancing chickens like he is the grim reaper," says Bubba, waving his arms, as if reinforcing his feelings by semaphore. "He says they are old and past it. And what's more, he's going to hold auditions to recruit a whole new troupe of Dixie Chickens."

Elvis tries to rationalise how someone as old as Greta Garbo, who retired more than 30 years ago, is suddenly back in demand as a hot property, while the Dixie Chickens, who always draw big crowds whenever they perform, are probably destined for some fried chicken fast food restaurant because they're too old. He supposes the relevance of age depends upon who you are and how you are perceived. It is a philosophical conundrum he must discuss later with his hairdresser, Larry Geller.

"Colonel, sir, please remember these chickens gave you your first big break in show business. How can you do this?" pleads his assistant.

"Well, not exactly these chickens. But yes, ones like them. Dancing chickens was my first act when I started out in carny. And nobody can deny what I've done for the cause of chickens in entertainment over the years. But from time to time, you've gotta renew the act."

The Colonel pushes back his yellow straw trilby and mops his brow with an old 'Loving You' handkerchief. "It's like this, boys. They are getting too old and their routines lack snap and sparkle. What the Dixie Chickens fans want, and what I intend to give them, is a younger, better looking, and higher kicking line-up of dancers." (What may not be apparent to the audience at their shows, since they are never allowed to get too close, is that the act consists of the chickens being put on a hot plate covered with straw. This causes them to hop about to various tunes, always beginning with their theme song 'Sweet Georgia Brown'.)

"How old is Greta Garbo? Yet she doesn't get recycled."

"Well, yes, but she lives a lot longer than a chicken."

Elvis tries to put it as delicately as possible – why does he need an audition. Don't all chickens look the same?

"Forgive me for saying this, son, but that's an amateur talking," replies Colonel Parker. "To a professional like me, and also their hard core fans, we can spot a Ginger Rogers straight away from a clodhopper. We need new blood. We've got to regenerate the act."

"But, Colonel Parker, sir, what will become of the existing Dixie Chickens?" asks Elvis.

Bubba, still clearly affected by the situation, interrupts. "He's talking about giving them to Minnie Mae for the stewpot. I do declare, can you imagine anything more hideous. One night soon we might all be sitting around the table at Graceland and fine dining on the Dixie Chickens. Eating our old friends. It doesn't bear thinking about."

Elvis wonders why they cannot be sent to one of those retirement homes for showbusiness people in the Catskills. There they'll be able to scratch around and roost in comfortable surroundings with other retired fellow performers, and from time to time people like the comedian Jackie Mason will come to entertain them. It all seems so simple and sensible to him.

"No No No No No," says the Colonel decisively, shaking his head for emphasis, and causing his chins to ripple like waves breaking on the seashore. "It's a question of economics, son. Those places are very expensive and we don't want a drain like that on our resources."

In the end, Elvis and Bubba get him to agree not to do anything too calamitous until he has spoken to them again.

"That heartless brute!" declares Elvis's wife, Priscilla, when she hears what is happening. "I'm going to tell that callous Colonel Parker we'll make a home for them right here at Graceland. It's the very least they deserve. Why I believe they'll be so happy they'll be laying lots of eggs in no time at all."

The Colonel has hired a hall for the auditions of the new Dixie Chickens and invites Elvis and Bubba to help with their advice and comments. Three chairs face a small stage on which there is a hotplate covered with straw where the chickens will perform their routines. Having sat down, Elvis wonders aloud if the days of music hall and variety are over.

Try telling that to Jack Benny and George Burns, replies the Colonel. He becomes, for him, quite wistful as he recalls how his career in showbusiness really began with his first troupe of Dixie Chickens. He is not just being sentimental when he says he intends to stay loyal to the act and its fans. There is still a good living to be had out there for this kind of entertainment.

"But it sure isn't rock 'n' roll," mutters Elvis.

The Colonel shouts to someone offstage to start the auditions. 'Sweet Georgia Brown' begins to play, a young guy with a few feathers stuck here and there to his dungarees, opens a basket and puts a chicken on the hot plate. It hops about and after 15 seconds the Colonel shouts "Next" and the chicken is scooped up and put back in another basket.

Ten or more chickens go through their 15-second slot before the Colonel suddenly leans forward in his chair and says, "I like this one." Elvis and Bubba ask what is so special about this bird. The Colonel points his cigar baton-like towards the stage and tells them, "Note the poise and the high kicks. This is a keeper," he calls out to the guy on the stage who puts it into a different basket, one that is kept for those that pass the audition.

"I've got a problem with the bird's colour. I prefer them to be white like Leghorns. Can we fix that?"

"Sure thing," comes the reply from the stage. "I've got some dye."

The straw on the hotplate is rearranged, more seed corn is strewn across it, and the next chicken begins its routine. Fifteen seconds later, the Colonel is calling out "Next!"

"Thank goodness I got a lot more than 15 seconds when I auditioned for Sam Phillips at Sun," remarks Elvis. "I reckon it was more like 15 days."

"Yes, son, it's a tough business," says the Colonel.

When Bubba asks what will become of the chickens that fail the auditions, he shakes his head, opens his arms wide, and tries on his regretful look. "That's showbiz," he sighs.

"What are we having for lunch today, Colonel? Roast chicken?" asks Elvis sarcastically.

Some time later, Colonel Parker receives a phone call from his old friend, Colonel Sanders, who wants to feature the Dixie Chickens in some new TV commercials and poster ads for his KFC restaurants; he wants to promote his new slogan 'high kickin' finger lickin' good'. But the new line-up is not ready yet, so it means a final curtain call for the old troupe before they move into their retirement hut in the grounds of Graceland and start work laying eggs for Priscilla.

To applause from everyone on the set at Paramount Studios, Greta Garbo makes her entrance as Queen Christina and sits down on the throne. "Grow a moustache and you'll look a lot like a film star I used to work with." she winks at Elvis, who is playing the role of her lover, Antonio, the Spanish envoy. She inhales deeply, flutters her fan, and declares that she is ready.

The director counts them in, the music backing track begins, and the Queen tells Antonio, "C'mon. let's start the party right now." She proceeds to tap dance her way down the steps from the throne.

"Cut!" The director calls through his megaphone. "Sorry, Elvis, but you need to move a bit quicker if you're gonna keep up and hit your spot. Congratulations Miss Garbo, that was terrific."

"Well you know they used to call me One-Take Greta," she grins. And Elvis can't help himself and starts laughing too.

Hal Wallis is awe-struck. Garbo laughs! A still picture of Elvis and Garbo laughing together on the set is going to be worth a fortune in advance publicity.

"You know, I didn't dance in my films but at friends' parties, up until quite recently, I used to dance a charleston to a tune called 'Sweet Georgia Brown'," she says. "It was my party trick and it would amaze my friends. They'd say I must be a spring chicken to do it."

Elvis smiles ruefully at her mention of the song and the comment 'spring chicken' while Bubba, fighting to control his emotion, blows his nose rather noisily.

Hal Wallis looks round to take in everyone on the set and says, "I'm sure everybody will join me in a round of applause for Miss Garbo. Who'd have thought you were such a good dancer. You continue to amaze your fans."

She smiles and graciously acknowledges their applause with a wave of her hand.

"Who would have thought I'd be making another movie after all this time. But thank you for giving me my comeback, I'm delighted, and I promise you all that I shall do my very, very best to earn every cent of my $10 million contract."

There is a loud crash like the noise of a heavy boulder falling off a cliff, caused by Colonel Parker slumping to the ground. Hal Wallis sends for the medics who waft smelling salts under his nose to bring him round; he can be heard faintly repeating, "ten million… ten million…"

It is a task that takes as much effort as getting a beached whale back into the sea, but eventually, the medics, with the help of some of the crew, manage to haul him up and sit him in a chair. Once he has stopped gasping for breath, he asks if he can borrow the director's megaphone. "Bubba. I need to talk to you. Right now."

Having sufficiently regained his composure, Colonel Parker is able to start puffing on a cigar; his assistant informs him that Miss Garbo has misread the number of noughts on the cheque.

"You mean there could be more?" he asks, with an edge of panic in his voice. "I sincerely hope you mean there are less".

"Less, Colonel. Exactly. And remember the cheque is drawn on your account at the Jefferson Davis Bank."

"Ah… of course. Well done, Bubba."

"Thank you, sir. I'm learning from The Master."

Ends

must have gone badly wrong. I expect there's a problem at the bank and at this very moment he's in his office trying to put it right."

"Oh, Elvis, stop kidding yourself," declares his wife, Priscilla, angrily. "It's his job to handle the money side of the business. Go and ask those poor folks down there outside the gates and they'll tell you he's not doing his job. Big time. I just hope they're not blaming you. Look how hard you work and all the money you make. Where does it all go? Why aren't these people being paid? It is an old problem that's come up before, and it needs to be sorted once and for all."

"I think you're being a bit hard on him, honey. I'm going to see him right now to get things put right."

He heads for his office but returns a few minutes later looking as if he has seen a ghost and clutching a sheet of paper that rustles in his shaking hand, like a leaf caught in a gust of wind.

"I f-f-found this in the C-C-Colonel's office," he stutters. He tells them that the note states that Colonel Parker has been kidnapped and will only be released upon the payment of a $2 million ransom.

"There's a sort of c-c-code at the b-b-bottom," he adds. "U O US. What does that mean?"

Priscilla snatches the piece of paper from him. "It means 'You Owe Us'. You can bet your bottom dollar he's been kidnapped by some of those folks down at the Music Gates who he owes money to. Good luck to them, I say. His chickens – and not the dancing ones – are coming home to roost."

Elvis suggests they should go inside, wait for the kidnappers to get in touch, and then decide what to do. But Priscilla offers a different approach. The man has to change his ways and this kidnapping may just be the perfect opportunity to teach him a lesson. Let him sweat it out for a few days and learn that everybody – from the kidnappers to all the suppliers he hasn't paid to Elvis himself – are sick of his cheapskate, chiselling ways.

Elvis pleads, "I hear what you say but we've got to remember that I owe him everything. I was driving a truck until he made me the biggest entertainer in the world."

"No, he didn't. That's all down to you and your talent, Elvis. Let the Colonel stew for a while in this mess of his own making. And then maybe he'll see the light and mend his ways."

"Are you boys in the Klan?" asks Colonel Parker.

"No, we're not. No sir, no," replies the leader of the kidnappers.

"I was wondering because it does look like it, what with you all wearing those King Biscuit flour bags over your heads, and those holes cut out for your eyes and your mouths. It's the sort of thing the Klan wear."

"It's just our disguise, Colonel. We're plain ordinary kidnappers trying as best we can to get the money that you've robbed from us over the years. We don't blame Elvis. We know you're the one who's supposed to pay the bills, at least when you're forced to. Like now."

They tell him that they are a sort of delegation of kidnappers appointed to represent everybody who is out of pocket. They've done their sums and when it is all added up they reckon they are all owed $2 million in total. The message is very simple: Pay up fast and in full or feel the heat of their anger. He suggests they might start by toasting his feet like marshmallows over a campfire, which brings an appreciative chuckle from the other two kidnappers.

It is a prospect that causes the Colonel to mop his brow, as he explains that something must have gone badly wrong at the long-established and normally so reliable Jefferson Davis Bank of Richmond. Just as soon as he is back at Graceland he will see that things are put right and all claims will be paid in full instantly. He and Elvis will put themselves through the pain barrier of writer's cramp signing all the cheques. So the best thing for all concerned is for them to release him straight away so he can start writing those cheques.

"Where are we by the way? Are we far from Memphis?" he inquires innocently. "How long before I can start paying you?"

They remind him that they may be only simple suppliers of goods and services to the Colonel and Elvis, and not considered worthy of being paid promptly for their work, but they are not fools.

As far as he is concerned he should know that he is being held somewhere safe, where nobody will ever think of looking for him. "So you could be hiding in a bank," says one of the other kidnappers and they all burst out laughing, causing loose flour from inside the bags that cover their heads to fall and form white dust on their shoulders.

"Let me make this plain, Colonel Parker, like the flour, ha ha ha – I wouldn't light a cigarette with one of your cheques," states the leader of the kidnappers. "This is a cash-only deal."

These things can take a little time to resolve so they might be able to amuse themselves while they wait with a friendly game of cards, suggests the Colonel, attempting to lighten the atmosphere. He makes a mess of shuffling the pack and tut-tuts at seeing the cards spill out of his hands and onto the table.

"You can see I'm a bit clumsy and I don't know much about cards. But I recall when I was a boy we used to play something at home called little old ladies double draw stud poker. Do you guys know it? Let me see if I can remember it…"

He is all fingers and thumbs and having made a hash of another shuffle he says they should play a few hands just to get the hang of it.

"See, you boys are already having fun and you're winning! Are you sure you've not played this before? I also seem to remember at home that sometimes, just to spice things up a little, we'd place a small bet on our hands…"

"There you go, you win again!" exclaims the Colonel. "By the way, if it gets too hot I don't mind if you boys take off the flour bags."

Elvis is with Priscilla and Bubba when the first call comes from the kidnappers. They want $1,990,000 in used, small denomination notes to release the Colonel unharmed. Elvis looks shocked and sits bolt upright. "What did you say?" he shouts. "Now just hold on there a minute. Did I hear you right? Yesterday the ransom was $2 million and today you're telling me it's $10,000 less. What is this – a special offer? Who am I dealing with – Walmart?"

From what she overhears, Priscilla is baffled as to what is going on and insists on taking the phone.

"I don't believe I am hearing this! You're telling me that you boys have lost $10,000 playing cards with Colonel Parker and he says to take it out of the ransom demand. Like it's a sort of credit note!"

She shakes her head in bewilderment as if trying to fathom some complex mathematical equation.

The rest of the instructions are that the money should be left in used notes in a laundry bag beneath a certain bench in W C Handy Park in Memphis. A time is given and the usual threats are made that if the police are informed then something very unpleasant will happen to Colonel Parker.

"How unpleasant?" she asks. "Would it be really nasty? Yes, it would be very very nasty, you say. Well, that's good to hear." As far as she is concerned things seem to have taken a turn for the better.

"Now listen to me very carefully, Mr. Kidnapper. We are not going to pay diddly squat. Not a single red cent. Have you got that! My suggestion is that you hang on to Colonel Parker and see if you can win back that $10,000."

She slams down the phone. Elvis looks distinctly worried about the consequences of these hardball tactics; he doesn't really want to face the future without his manager. In need of some comfort, he sends Charlie to find a box of donuts.

There's another phone call the next day from the kidnappers informing Elvis that the ransom is reduced by another $25,000, the result of further losses from playing poker with Colonel Parker. The arrangements for the delivery of the money – now $1,965,000 – remain the same, as does the imminent threat to his wellbeing.

"Can I ask you a question, Elvis? Is he lucky at cards? Or is he a cheat?" inquires the leader of the kidnappers.

"My advice is to watch him like a hawk and stop playing poker with him," states Elvis. "Play happy families instead. I mean, what can go wrong playing that?"

Once again Priscilla, who is becoming increasingly agitated, takes the phone from him and tells the kidnapper, "Have you finished because I am looking at my watch and I need to leave for an important business meeting. And oh, by the way, we're not paying any ransom money."

The kidnappers go into a huddle, muttering to each other under their flour bag disguises. They are puzzled why Elvis is not paying up right away to secure the Colonel's release; after all, that's what people are supposed to do when there's been a kidnapping. It doesn't seem to make any sense – don't they want him back?

It is something that is also baffling the Colonel. Not only is it taking a long time to secure his release but what is really worrying him is that Priscilla is also involved in the negotiations. That does not bode well given his relationship with her. He buys time by explaining that refusing to pay is a classic negotiating tactic in kidnappings, and anyway, even Elvis doesn't have a couple of million dollars lying around the house in spare change.

"He'll be frantic with worry," he tries to reassure them. "And so will my network of business associates. They won't want to see anything happen to the good ole Colonel. I bet people like Hal Wallis, Hank Snow, and Tommy Sands will doing all they can to help Elvis get the ransom together as fast as possible."

In the meantime, while they wait, he suggests another game of poker, but the kidnappers refuse, saying they are going to stick to happy families.

"I've never heard of it. You learn something new every day, so thanks, boys. Go ahead and teach me how to play it."

Beneath the King Biscuit flour bags, the kidnappers are soon far from happy. Smiles become scowls.

When they first begin playing happy families, they are winning, so they think they will ride the tide of their luck by gambling on the hands. Something they promised themselves they will not do anymore. But with the Colonel struggling to collect so much as one family, he is there for the taking. They decide to go for the kill in order to recoup their losses.

But as the Colonel remarks later, "It's funny how quickly the tide can turn."

He lays down his cards and says, "Look I've got all the Baker family now and most of the other cards, so does that mean I've won again?"

The kidnappers groan and toss their hands into the centre of the table.

"It must be beginner's luck. One more hand before lunch?" Colonel Parker suggests.

Priscilla takes the latest call from the kidnappers. "Just a moment while I check my diary. Now let me see... yes, I can give you a five-minute window, so best to talk quickly."

Having listened for a short while she replies, "How's what ransom coming along? Oh, that ransom... Do you know it has clean slipped my mind. I'll put Elvis on the line and he can give you an update."

She and Elvis have come up with a ruse to turn the screw and jack up the Colonel's anxiety levels by letting him know how well things are going in his absence.

"We've been really busy here at Graceland," Elvis tells the kidnappers, "what with finalising plans for my first European tour and then a musical on Broadway... You say you've lost another $15,000 playing happy families with him. How did that happen? And you watched him like a hawk... that's a helluva run of bad luck..."

"About the ransom – how much is it?... $2 million less the $50,000 you've now lost playing cards... We'll get on it right away... Sorry, I've got to go. I've got Carnegie Hall on the other line."

Talking things over later with Priscilla and Bubba, he says that once Colonel Parker hears about these so-called plans that he knows nothing about he'll start to panic. And then he'll think about all the deals he could be missing out on, and panic some more.

"And all this is happening when he's not the one taking care of business. He's gonna be madder than a wasp trapped in a jar," laughs Elvis.

They agree that they have left him for long enough with the kidnappers and perhaps he might have learned a lesson about the damage that not paying bills on time can cause to people's lives as well as to Elvis's good name.

They find Colonel Parker sitting on a bench in W C Handy Park with a piece of paper pinned to the lapel of his jacket on which is listed the names of all the suppliers who are owed money. He seems tense and nervous, and that is understandable given what he must have gone through.

But it soon emerges that what is really worrying him is not the kidnapping ordeal but the plans for the European tour and the Broadway musical that were mentioned in phone calls to the kidnappers and in which he has had no involvement. Will they make any money? What might have been missed in the small print of the contracts? The merchandising rights?

And the biggest fear of all that's gnawing away at him is that Elvis, Bubba, and Priscilla might have made a good job of it without him.

He tells them he needs to get to work right away. It may not be too late for him to salvage what he can from the commitments they have made. But they assure him that all plans are put on hold until he is back behind his desk at Graceland.

Elvis and Bubba previously met the kidnappers, still wearing their King Biscuit flour bags over their heads, at a remote spot on the Natchez Trace Parkway to give them the $2 million, along with their heartfelt apologies. He'd got the money from the International Hotel in Las Vegas as an advance against his next season of shows. For Elvis, it is no problem, they say. How quickly does he need it? Now? No problem.

"There's no hard feelings, boys," Elvis tells the kidnappers. "It's just a pity that you had to kidnap the Colonel to get the money you're owed. But I guess you were desperate and I'm sorry. I hope that he has learned his lesson and things will be different."

"I thought you'd like to know that we handed over the ransom money – all $2 million of it – so that all the suppliers who were owed money can be paid," Elvis tells Colonel Parker.

"Who? Oh them," he replies, as if he has been reminded of some minor domestic detail.

"I let them keep the $50,000 they lost playing cards with you. I read a story once, or was it a painting I saw, called 'Massacre of the Innocents'. Those poor kidnappers had no idea what they were getting into."

"Don't you worry, son," blusters Colonel Parker. "I'll get it back – every single cent of it."

Elvis and Bubba look at each other, despair etched on their faces. Will he never learn? Does he not realise what he did was wrong and why it ended up with him being kidnapped?

"Oh all right then, I agree. We should pay these people quickly," he announces, his jowelled face illuminated like a heavily stubbled light bulb.

Elvis and Bubba exchange glances and smiles as if to say 'Eureka'.

"And here's what we are going to do," he continues, smiling to himself. "In return for being paid within 28 days, they agree to give us a discount of say, 10 or 15 per cent off the bill. Or maybe we can squeeze them for 20 per cent. What do you think?"

He is really pleased with himself and his latest scheme; the Colonel is back on top and he gives a Groucho Marx-style celebratory twirl to his cigar.

"Oh no," groans Elvis, who is asking himself if this is the brutal truth that he must live with: that it may not be possible to teach an old dog, and certainly not one as old as Colonel Parker, a new trick. All that has happened during the past few days, and some of it with Elvis's connivance, was in the hope that he would learn the error of his ways. But he bounces right back like a jack-in-the-box. The man is beyond redemption.

Ends

4. The Queen and the Laird of Prestwick

"Let me get this straight. You are telling me that Elvis has had an invitation to go to Scotland from the Queen of England! How the hell did this happen, Bubba?" complains Colonel Tom Parker to his assistant. "All mail is supposed to come through this office. That's the system. That's how we manage things."

"I cannot understand it either," pleads Bubba. "The only thing I can think of is that we somehow got bypassed and the invitation was delivered personally to Elvis and it got through the system that way."

"Perhaps it was one of those footmen that work for the Queen at Buckingham Palace who brought it," he suggests.

"A footman, boy! Have you gone mad?! Have you seen what those guys wear? Dressed like that one of them wouldn't last five minutes on the streets of Memphis."

Nevertheless, his assistant cannot help admiring the smooth quality of the envelope and the red seal on the back that had to be broken to open it. Meanwhile, the Colonel has become so agitated that his head has assumed the look of a plum tomato simmering in a pan – bright red and very hot. He alternates between mopping his brow with a 'Loving You' souvenir bandana and puffing furiously on his Walmart special offer corona cigar as he attempts to quell the rising panic. With any luck, Elvis won't reply until he has checked with him first, but there is always that very slim chance that he may have done something irrevocable, such as mention it to his wife, Priscilla.

Instinctively, he wants to reach for the gaming machine beside his desk to feel the calming reassurance of the lever in his hand and the joy that might follow if he were to win big; to date, he never has, despite all the hours he spends tinkering with the machine. It is an interesting thought, but Thomas Edison probably spent a lot less time inventing the electric light bulb than the Colonel has in attempting to 'doctor' his one-arm bandit.

As a result of all the hours he spends pumping away on the lever, which the Colonel claims helps him to think big business thoughts, he has developed a repetitive strain injury in his right arm, and now, according to Dr. Nick, Elvis's personal physician, tennis elbow in his left. Sitting under a tree looking at apples used to work for some old scientist in England, reflects the Colonel, so why shouldn't he have a gaming machine in his office to double up as his amanuensis and universal panacea? But tempting though it is, and much as he wants to, he decides against putting himself through the pain barrier and elects to leave it alone.

This is a crisis which he must deal with immediately, so he regretfully needs to postpone a visit to the International Hotel in Las Vegas. His plan was to stay for a few days in his usual suite while he negotiated the terms of Elvis's next residency. Perhaps he will be able to shoehorn in additional matinee performances as well as the usual twice-nightly shows. That should generate a lot of extra dollars, as well as an upgrade in his suite and his gambling credit limit. During his stay there will be the opportunity to try his luck at roulette, dice, poker, the slots – the world is his oyster.

The invitation, which is on a thick white card with gold edging and a beautiful manuscript print, together with an accompanying handwritten letter from the Queen, travelled to the USA via the diplomatic bag, and was then delivered to Graceland by a diplomatic attaché. Since then, they have hardly left Priscilla's hand, she is so excited. The one exception, which she immediately regrets, is when she showed them to Elvis's grandmother, Minnie Mae, who at the time was in the kitchen preparing a hogs feet stew for dinner. She asks to have a look at them and leaves a greasy thumb print on the invitation.

Priscilla's intention is to have them framed, but for now, they stand propped up on a mantelpiece in the lounge, illuminated by a spotlight from the ceiling.

The letter from Her Majesty says how sorry she is that Mr. Presley was unable to take part in last year's Royal Variety Performance because of his indisposition as reported by his manager. She says that Tennessee swamp fever sounds very unpleasant, requiring as it does a long period of quarantine. But she hopes that the rash and the swellings have now cleared up and Mr. Presley is feeling much better.

When Priscilla subsequently tackles the Colonel about the letter, saying that she was unaware that Elvis had caught Tennessee swamp fever, he assures her that this was the diagnosis of Dr. Nick. "That fool couldn't diagnose a common cold," she declares and storms out of his office. The truth of the matter, she believes, is that for whatever reason, the Colonel doesn't want them to go, but he won't stop them this time, no sir. She has made her mind up. They are going to Scotland and will meet the Queen.

The invitation is to attend the Royal Highland Games at Braemar. It is addressed to Elvis as Honorary Chief of the Clan Presley and Laird of All the Glens of Prestwick. Also invited are the Lady of the Chief of the Clan – Priscilla – his piper and six of his ghillies or retainers who, as well as waiting on them, will be expected, as is the custom, to compete in the Highland Games.

Edith Head, the multi-Oscar-winning costume designer has been flown in from Hollywood and is sitting with Priscilla in the living room at Graceland sketching designs for the dresses and outfits that she will wear. In Priscilla's opinion, if Elvis is the King of Rock and Roll, then she must be the Queen, so she wants to look suitably regal.

She tells Edith Head, "Remember, we two Queens are going to be spending a lot of time together, you know, chatting and watching the shows. I need to look stylish, chic, and classy. Best of all, I'd like people to be scratching their heads and saying to themselves: Which one is Queen Elizabeth and which one is Queen Priscilla?"

She suggests that Elizabeth Taylor or Audrey Hepburn should be her role model in terms of how to look. Edith Head's face does not betray what she is thinking as she draws another outfit on her sketchpad, but it is certainly not of Audrey Hepburn or Elizabeth Taylor. The outfits should feature some reference to the Presley tartan, recommends Priscilla, but it should be understated. Perhaps no more than a small bow or a brooch. Then she suddenly remembers, "And don't forget a tiara."

"What about some lucky white heather? Do you think you'll need it," wonders Edith Head.

Priscilla declines, not sure if it is supposed to be a joke.

Elsewhere in the Jungle Room, Elvis is telling Bernard Lansky that he will not under any circumstances wear a kilt. He does not understand what possesses Scotsmen to wear them, especially when Scotland is supposed to be so cold.

Bernard Lansky, who has been designing Elvis's clothes since he first found fame at Sun Records, says not to worry. What he has in mind for Elvis is trews, which is what they call trousers in Scotland. However, he will give them a modern twist in a hipster style with big flares, and they will be done in the Presley tartan. He is proposing a tight-fitting black jacket with gold buttons and a high stiff collar, a cape with a picture of the Monarch of the Glen – note the royal touch, he tells Elvis – a lace cravat and a leopard skin sporran.

"By the time we're finished, you're going to look more Scottish than Bob Roy," he asserts with a confident flourish of his tape measure around Elvis's waist. He makes a show of holding up the tape and inspecting it and then asking Elvis if he is losing weight while still managing to keep a straight face.

"Do you think I should dye my hair ginger to fit in with all the other Scottish people when we go to the Royal Highland Games?" Elvis asks his hairdresser, Larry Geller.

Still wearing his clan chief highland outfit, he turns slowly from side to side as he studies himself in the gilt-framed chevalier mirror, while unseen by Elvis, his hairdresser tries to recover from being stabbed through the heart by the words 'ginger hair'.

Fighting hard to suppress the tears, Larry Geller replies, "Your natural hair colour is... er... black and that is how your fans and your Presley clanspeople will want to see you."

He asks Elvis to take a seat while he styles his hair. "Of course, hair dye is quite unnecessary for you," he adds with a cough. "But we need the merest hint of a highlight here and there."

As he works away, Larry Geller remarks that he has been doing some research on Elvis's links with Scotland. He has discovered that an Andrew Presley was married at Lonmay Church in Aberdeenshire in 1713, but what is really interesting is that his son, also called Andrew, left Scotland after the Jacobite Rebellion in 1745 and went to live in South Carolina.

"Maybe he had to escape because he was friends with Bonnie Prince Charlie and Flora MacDonald," he ponders as he primps away. "It is a sort of royal connection that goes way back."

"Yea," says Elvis, becoming quite animated. "And what if, when they were on the run, the three of them went to Prestwick, the home of Clan Presley, and my ancestor helped them escape over the sea to Skye. Perhaps Andrew Presley was in the boat with Bonnie Prince Charlie and Flora. This is history, this is drama."

"You know what," adds Larry Geller, as he manoeuvres the mirror so that Elvis can admire his handiwork, "it would make a great TV programme. You could visit all these places we're talking about, chat to folks about this history, and sing some songs. I think it would really work."

"Larry, I love it. Och aye," laughs Elvis.

At Buckingham Palace, the Queen's Private Secretary reports that as regards the guests invited to the Royal Highland Games, they have now received an acceptance from Mr. and Mrs. Elvis Presley.

"Who?" she inquires, as she finishes her cup of tea and puts the uneaten biscuits away in a tupperware container.

"I believe he is a popular entertainer, Your Majesty," he replies.

"You mean like Chick Murray or Kenneth McKellar?"

"I'm not sure, Your Majesty. But you're right, there is a Scottish connection. The invitation was extended to him in his capacity as Honorary Chief of Clan Presley and Laird of the All the Glens of Prestwick."

"Will he have far to come?"

"Yes, Your Majesty. He resides in the United States, and he will be accompanied by Mrs. Presley, his piper, and the requisite number of ghillies."

"Let's put them in Prince Philip's group. He's always very good with these sort of showbusiness types. I'm sure his sense of humour will appeal to them."

Charlie Hodge, Elvis's old friend, gofer, and chief booster is desperately trying to whip up enthusiasm for the trip to the Royal Highland Games but there is so much lethargy in the Jungle Room that it resembles a retirement home for giant sloths. But to be fair, the guys have just finished a snack lunch of takeaway pizzas and Krispy Kreme donuts and that has probably worn them out.

Red West's only contribution before falling asleep, with a can of beer tilting precariously in his hand, is that they should all wear 'Team Elvis' t-shirts. Charlie points out that they are expected to wear traditional highland outfits and compete in some of the games; this produces a chorus of groans.

"Elvis insists!" he shouts over the hubbub and the murmurs gradually die down as he tries to give them his hard man stare. He consults his notes and says that Elvis suggests Lamar Fike should be in the haggis eating contest and therefore he must be their best bet for a win of any kind. And with him weighing more than 20 stone, he is also a must to be the anchor in the tug-of-war team.

Red has been entered in the stag carcass carrying race, he reports.

"You said they were games, but these sound like hard work," complains Red between yawns.

Charlie says he has put himself down for the caber tossing event. He does not know what a caber is, but he assumes it is the Scottish word for a pancake since it involves being tossed.

"Good ole Charlie. He always gets the easy ticket," sneers Sonny West.

Elvis, accompanied by Charlie, has gone to see Colonel Parker in his office to tell him about his idea for a documentary based on his Scottish ancestor and the '45 Jacobite Rebellion.

The Colonel, who is busy winnowing suppliers' invoices and filling a wastepaper basket with those that don't pass muster, pauses to jab his cigar in Charlie's direction and says, "What's he doing here? The office is perfectly clean."

He makes an exaggerated display of thinking deeply. "Hmm, let me think. Yes, I've got it. It's a film about household cleaning products! Ha, ha, ha."

But the Colonel has misjudged the mood; Elvis sits still and stony-faced until he stops chuckling to himself and indicates for him to begin. The basic outline concerns Elvis's ancestor, Andrew Presley, and his involvement with Bonnie Prince Charlie and the '45 rebellion, their flight across the heather, always evading the Redcoat soldiers in the nick of time, and how he eventually helped the Prince escape before he himself fled to America.

"So it is a sort of road trip movie, but shot in tartan," smirks Colonel Parker. "I reckon the whole thing could be done on the Paramount studio lot."

"No, sir. This will be a serious documentary that will be done on location. In the real places and not some backlot. This is my family's history, it's exciting, it's all true and I want to do it!"

"Documentaries don't make money," is the rejoinder from the Colonel.

Elvis disagrees and says it makes perfect sense for movie producer Hal Wallis to send a film crew with him to Scotland while he and Priscilla are at the Royal Highland Games. As a clincher, he adds that he may be able to persuade the Queen to take part and give an interview since she is a descendant of Bonnie Prince Charlie. What with her participation in the documentary and a couple of traditional Scottish songs that he'll sing, the project cannot fail.

"Oh boy, this story is so good Errol Flynn must be grumbling in his grave that he's not around to do it," asserts Charlie.

Colonel Parker looks at him with what he hopes is his most withering sneer.

"Anyway, Priscilla has already booked the tickets," Elvis tells him. "She insists that we're definitely going because there's no way she is going to miss out on meeting the Queen."

Has the world suddenly gone mad? Because this sort of thing is not supposed to happen, ponders the Colonel. He is the one who takes care of business – not Elvis and Priscilla.

This whole Scottish adventure is fraught with danger. The prospect of Elvis, accompanied by Priscilla, the Memphis Mafia, and a film crew roaming around Scotland, as well as meeting the Queen of England, without his hands-on supervision, would be a complete abdication of his management role. It really cannot be permitted.

Then there is the issue of his status as an American citizen. Over the years there have been a number of ugly stories that allege that as a teenager he illegally entered the United States after fleeing Holland to escape a murder charge. He has never held a US passport and that is why, it is claimed, he never leaves the country – because he might never be allowed back in or he might be arrested on an international warrant.

"No, Bubba, I can't make the trip to Scotland because I have some very important meetings that cannot be put off," he tells his assistant.

Bubba looks hard at the Colonel and smells a trilby-wearing, cigar-smoking, shifty-looking rat. "What meetings are these?" he asks. "There's nothing in the diary."

"They're top secret. All I can say is that they're with Hal Wallis and RCA and are absolutely crucial to Elvis's future."

"Then why don't you let me go to Scotland with them?"

The Colonel smiles sadly, wrings his hands, and says that it is a very kind offer. But the trip cannot go ahead. It is a situation he bitterly regrets. (How he wishes there was a string of onions in the drawer of his desk so that he could put them around his neck and shed a convincing tear.) For something so important as this, he needs to be there. Without his on-the-spot expertise, there is so much that could go wrong. It simply would not be fair to his assistant to put him in such a difficult position.

"For everyone's sake, this visit to Scotland simply cannot go ahead," he adds with a regretful sigh.

Now, of course, he needs to find a way of putting a stop to it.

Priscilla finds a new invitation propped up in the kitchen; it is to a Presley family hoedown. There are two things that she notices right away. Unlike all communications from the other members of the Presley family, the invitation is well written and free of spelling mistakes and greasy marks. Secondly, it is due to take place on the same weekend that she and Elvis go to Scotland. It will be held in Tupelo, Elvis and Priscilla are the guests of honour, and every single Presley family member from far and wide will be there.

She is in no doubt that the planned hoedown is real, but because of the timing and how it seems to have arrived out of the blue, she is deeply suspicious as to who is behind it. And why.

She remembers the last one they went to a couple of years ago that, for her, was as full of horrors as an Edgar Allan Poe story. Various distant cousins turned up in their dungarees and jigged barefoot in the dirt to jug band music played on an old wind-up gramophone with a big horn, the sort the dog used to listen to. One of the first things that happened was to set up a still.

Elvis was persuaded to take part in a game called 'catch the greasy pig'. And once it was caught, it was butchered by his grandmother, Minnie Mae, and put on a spit for a hog roast. There were hoots of laughter and much slapping of thighs when Priscilla asked for a green salad instead of a heaped plate of pork. The whole thing was ghastly. She half-wonders to herself how they would have fared in an audition for the 'Deliverance' movie.

Elvis warned her many years before about the eccentricities of their Presley-Hood kinfolk. Her first experience was going to the funeral of Enoch Hood, a cousin of Minnie Mae's, and she questioned why a cow was standing at the back of the church.

"Why, Priscilla, that be Daisy an' she's the chief mourner," Minnie Mae told her. "Ah do declare Cousin Enoch wus closer to her than anybody else in the whole world. She's bin a-left ter me in his will to take care of."

Priscilla insists that Elvis should accompany her to confront the Colonel and tell him as forcefully as possible that they are determined to go to Scotland. The last place on earth where she wants to go is the family hoedown.

She nods to Elvis to take his cue. He looks down, shuffles, fiddles with the fringes of his jumpsuit, and finally mumbles, "Yes, Colonel Parker, like Priscilla says, we do want to go to Scotland."

But already she is losing patience and points a forefinger with its stiletto of a long red nail at the Colonel and tells him, "No one ever, and I mean ever, ignores a personal invitation from Her Majesty the Queen. We will be there like ambassadors representing the United States of America. That's how important this is."

There is a long pause as the Colonel sits back in his chair and takes a couple of reflective puffs on his cigar before telling them they have to see the bigger picture.

"Oh sure, we see it all right, don't we Elvis?"

He nods his head in agreement.

"He'll be there as the head of Clan Presley and the Laird of Prestwick, mingling with the Queen and all the other chiefs. And this trip will give Elvis the chance to find out about his family history and make a documentary. It is very, very important to him. And it will also be a holiday for us and Lord knows, we need one."

"Colonel, I want to go back my roots in Scotland where it all began for the Presleys," adds Elvis.

Colonel Parker smiles apologetically as if to say what can I do? Yes, it would be wonderful if they could all go to Scotland, himself included. But when it leaks out to the press, what will his fans think if Elvis is seen to be dumping his entire family and the special party they have organised for him to undertake some jaunt in a foreign country. It will be a PR calamity because family must always come first.

Priscilla wonders how the information would leak out, and the Colonel shrugs and says, "Who knows?"

She looks hard at him and if looks could kill, he would be dying a horrible death. She asks him, as Elvis's manager, to contact the Queen to see if she can postpone the Royal Highland Games for a week so that they can attend.

"I don't think she does that kind of thing. But of course, I'll try."

That'll be the day, she thinks. As they leave his office, Priscilla stops and turns to him. "By the way, Elvis insists that you attend the family hoedown, to take care of business and, of course, to join in all the fun and games. I'm sure you'll particularly enjoy catching the greasy hog."

Later, Elvis tells Charlie everything that happened in the Colonel's office and how disappointed he and Priscilla are that they can't go to Scotland as planned. The Colonel says he will try and get the Royal Highland Games postponed for a week, but it is more likely that hogs will pass over Graceland in a fly-past. He is dejected and, what is so unlike him, he is not showing any interest in his de luxe whoppa meal deal pizza. Charlie, his oldest friend, has never seen him like this and wonders what he can do to lift him out of this melancholia.

Charlie is saddened too because in preparation for the tournament he has been spending a lot of time in the kitchen making pancakes and 'tossing the cabers', as he believes they are called in Scotland.

Is there anything at all that he can do to help Elvis? he ponders and then – Eureka! – he has an idea.

When nobody is about, Charlie picks up a phone and dials.

"Hiya, ah mean hello, is that Buckingham Palace that I'm talking to?"

"No, it's the Buckingham Arms, Westminster," is the response from the landlord.

"Well, I'm wondering now if I've got the right place? I don't suppose the Queen is there?" asks Charlie.

"I'll just go and have a look... Yes, she's in the snug," the landlord tells him, deciding to play along for a while. After all, it might make an entertaining story to tell his customers on an otherwise dull day.

"Thank you very much. I'd be very grateful if I could just have a word with her."

"I'll just go and ask... she says she's right in the middle of a game of cribbage. That's her calling out 'one for his nob'."

"Right, well I certainly don't want to disturb her when she's busy, but please pass on a message. Say this is Charlie, Elvis's friend. And Elvis would be really, really grateful if she can delay her Royal Highland Games in Scotland for a week or two so he can be there. It's very important. He wants to be there and doesn't want to let her down."

"Elvis, you say. Right you are, sir. Postpone the games because Elvis is coming. That certainly is important. I'll go and tell her right away. Consider it done."

The landlord turns to the two men in the bar and says, "You're not going to believe this, but that was the weirdest phone call I've ever had."

Ends

5. The Millions of Dollars Quartet

As mistakes go, it was a big one. Perhaps not like the time that the Decca record label turned down The Beatles. Or the scale of when Archduke Franz Ferdinand's car took the wrong turning in Sarajevo and his assassination led to the start of the First World War. But the consequence of this mistake is that Minnie Mae, Elvis's grandmother, and rock and roller Jerry Lee Lewis, are now locked up in adjoining cells in a police station in Memphis.

"Y'all ain't gonna beat no confession outta me," she shouts as she stands there gripping the bars of her cell. "Ah ain't afeared. Take me down ter Parchman Farm. Jest strap the picker sack across mah back cuz ah ain't fergot how ter pick cotton. No sir. Don't you worry none about me, ah can do mah time."

"You tell 'em, Minnie Mae," grins Jerry Lee Lewis. "I'm going to be pleading with the judge to send Ole Jerry Lee straight to Folsom Prison. Why then I can show them boys in that there gaol how to put on a real show – something that'll tear up the joint. Not like that lily-livered album from Johnny Cash. The Killer will give 'em the real stuff – a rock 'n' roll inferno, yessir."

The Chief of Police is in a panic; having Jerry Lee Lewis in the cells is one thing; after all, he has been there before – but Elvis's grandmother! He is shouting for someone to get Colonel Tom Parker there as fast as possible to sort out this mess before word of it gets out and finishes his career. Elvis's grandmother in his cells. It's his worst nightmare. His prospects for future employment would be a lot less damaging if they'd arrested Mother Teresa.

He winces as he hears Minnie Mae in the cells yelling that she's not worried about doing time on the chain gang.

"Where's Colonel Parker?" he calls out in desperation. "Is he on his way yet? And why in hell's name were they arrested? Did anybody die?"

"No Chief, but it was like the Gunfight at the OK Corral. We had to."

And yet it had all started so differently…

Colonel Parker is in his office at Graceland, reflectively puffing on a cigar he got for free at the gas station when he filled up his car. The meeting is to talk through plans with Elvis for a short tour between seasons at the International Hotel in Las Vegas. But it is a desultory affair with nothing worthwhile being suggested or agreed upon; Elvis seems more interested in his bumper bucket of chocolate coated popcorn and a chocolate milkshake, and Bubba, the Colonel's assistant, is yawning as if it were siesta time. The meeting is going nowhere. But then, out of the blue, Elvis says he has an idea.

"Careful, son," says the Colonel. "Remember our deal. You do the singing and I do the thinking."

Elvis shrugs and resumes eating his popcorn, but Bubba, who has been fighting to suppress a yawn, proposes they should hear what he has to say, after all, nothing is happening so they have nothing to lose.

"Why Colonel Parker, sir, do you happen to remember that one time at Sun when Sam Phillips got to recording me and Jerry Lee and Carl Perkins and Johnny Cash when we were singing around the piano in the studio? We were just fooling around, mainly doing old gospel songs, but Sam kept the tape running. At the time he called it the Million Dollar Quartet. Now all I'm saying is that what if the four of us could get together again and do a short tour?"

Slowly, like a hippopotamus emerging from a deep mudhole, the Colonel struggles to his feet from behind his desk and lets out a loud whoop. He laughs and hops about on his feet, causing the office to shake, and Bubba thinks he may actually be trying to dance a jig, causing the cigar ash that has been accumulating down the front of his Hawaiian shirt to fall to the ground like a light powder of snow.

"Elvis, son, what an idea! It's brilliant!" He pushes his yellow straw trilby to the back of his head and mops his face with an old 'Loving You' souvenir handkerchief.

There is more laughter and hopping about and then suddenly he falls back into his chair with the force of a tidal wave hitting a harbour wall. He looks happy but he is breathing hard and his face is as red as a split watermelon. Between every gasp for breath, he repeats the word 'brilliant'.

It must be years since he has moved so quickly and expended so much energy in so short a time. The 'Dead March' from 'Saul' would be a lively tempo for the Colonel's normal speed of movement. In a race with a sloth, you would not want to bet on the Colonel.

Elvis is concerned enough to go over and offer him a drink of his milkshake while Bubba rings Dr. Nick, Elvis's personal physician, and tells him to come quickly because they are worried about the Colonel's health.

"What is the matter with him?" he asks when he has arrived. "Is it his stomach? What has he been eating? Does he need an enema?" He opens his mobile dispensary, which is a suitcase on wheels with a big red cross and removes a long rubber hose. The Colonel begins to panic and looks around his office for a means of escape.

"I'm not sure but I think he's been dancing and he's had a funny turn," Bubba reports.

"My goodness me, the Colonel dancing! Can this be true? No wonder he is unwell. I bet he hasn't danced since the great days of the Cotton Club." He says he will give him some pills to settle him down and also leave a constipation unblocker linctus just in case. He will go back to his surgery to write some prescriptions and come back and check how he is again tomorrow.

Seeing Dr. Nick leave his office and towing away his mobile dispensary is enough of a tonic for the Colonel. He has a score to settle with Scatter, Elvis's pet chimpanzee, so he knows just what to do with the linctus when the opportunity arises. The Million Dollar Quartet, he thinks to himself. Anything which contains the word 'million' is music to the Colonel. By the time he has finished doing deals for an album, a movie tie-in, and the truck-loads of merchandising for which he will need to contact his suppliers in Bangladesh and Soweto to get them working around the clock as soon as possible, they should be looking at the $20 Million Quartet at the very least.

Elvis's idea has given him a new lease on life. He's refreshed, back at the top of his game. Maybe his luck has changed as well.

He walks over to the gaming machine that he keeps in his office and pulls the lever. Up pop into the window one and then two gold discs, each bearing an image of Elvis's face. And then comes the third one with the word 'Loser'.

The Colonel shrugs his shoulders and says, "Never mind. I was that close." Which he demonstrates by showing the tiny gap between his forefinger and thumb.

Bubba tells Colonel Parker that the Million Dollar Quartet tour is doomed to fail simply because it will take more than a year just to arrange to get Elvis and the other three in the same room at the same time. Like Elvis, they are constantly touring and performing, and finding a spot in their diaries will be like looking for a ham sandwich at a bar mitzvah.

"They'll be here any day now," he declares, tapping the side of his nose with his cigar (thankfully unlit).

"Pardon me for mentioning it, sir, but it'll be downright impossible. You're going to need handcuffs to get them all here."

And, of course, Bubba is right that it does prove to be tough. On being told that the Colonel is on the phone, Carl Perkins, Johnny Cash, and Jerry Lee Lewis simply refuse to take the calls. It is like being told the Grim Reaper is on the line; you really don't want to hear what he has to say. They know the Colonel of old and want nothing to do with yet another dodgy deal that he'll be trying to sell. Over the years, their fingers have not just been burned by Colonel Parker, they have caught fire. "Tell him Ole Jerry Lee is fully booked for the next five years," he informs his own manager. And that's typical of the replies of the other two.

But the Colonel is limpet-like in his persistence, knowing that if he can convince Jerry Lee then the others will follow suit. By pretending to be a representative of the Jack Daniel Distillery with a complimentary gift of a case of whiskey, he and Elvis manage to get admitted to his dressing room at one of his country music shows. Once he gets over the double shock – it's the Colonel and there is no whiskey as promised – Jerry Lee holds a Bible aloft and quotes, staring all the time at Colonel Parker, "And I looked, and behold a pale horse: and his name that sat on him was Death, and Hell followed with him. And power was given unto them over the fourth part of the earth, to kill with sword, and with hunger, and with death, and with the beasts of the earth." It does seem incomprehensible that the wildest man in rock and roll was once a student at a bible college in Texas, but it is a fact. He also believes that he has a greater knowledge of the Bible than his cousin, the Rev Jimmy Lee Swaggart, the TV evangelist.

He lays down the soft black leather-bound Bible, takes a revolver from a drawer, lays it on top of the Bible, and says, "Yes?"

Elvis asks him how he is enjoying playing the chicken wire roadhouse circuit, singing songs like 'She Even Woke Me Up To Say Goodbye', and sitting in a dressing room that looks like it is usually used as a beer cellar. "Don't you miss the good old days of rock and roll?"

"It don't matter none," he replies. "Ole Jerry Lee just loves to play and perform and folks always wanna hear The Killer. And I'm getting well paid." Then he looks hard at the Colonel, puts his hand on top of the revolver and the Bible, and adds, "And there's never any funny business with the money, you know what I mean."

"Talking of money, I've got just three words to say to you, Jerry Lee."

"Well, I've got three as well, and they're 'go to hell'."

"Here's my three words: millions of dollars."

"Just run that by me again."

"Millions of dollars."

"Now Elvis, we've known each other a long, long time. I trust you. You tell Ole Jerry Lee this ain't a pail of pigswill."

"First, this is my idea. You can hand me that Bible and I'll swear it is for real. The Colonel is right. We are talking about making millions of dollars. Just listen to what we have to say."

The next day, to Bubba's amazement, Jerry Lee Lewis, Johnny Cash, and Carl Perkins are sitting with Elvis in the Colonel's office at Graceland, talking about the Million Dollar Quartet shows.

"Now, before we get down to the details, tell The Killer and the rest of the boys just what this whole shooting match is gonna be worth," says Jerry Lee.

Colonel Parker draws on his cigar and holds their gaze for upwards of 20 seconds, building up towards his revelation. He gives a slight shrug and says casually, "$20 million and rising. Come back to Graceland next week and I'll have added another $10 million."

"Hee Hah!" hoots Jerry Lee, running his hand through his long, curly hair and slapping his thigh. "Well, I'm saying let's get going right now."

"It's one for the money, two for the show, three to get ready, now go Colonel go," sings Carl Perkins.

"What do you think, Johnny?" asks Elvis.

Johnny Cash lights another cigarette from the butt of the one he has just finished and nods his head.

"I see you're in a chatty mood," comments the Colonel ironically.

Johnny taps the brim of his black Stetson hat with his forefinger and blows a smoke ring. "Yep," he says.

The meeting goes very smoothly, with an agreement being reached quickly on how to split up the proceeds: everything from the shows, the album, and the movie will be divided equally four ways between them. The lion's share of the merchandising will go to the Colonel since, as he argues, he is doing everything else apart from singing on stage. He points out it will be billed as a once-in-a-lifetime tour but he will make sure that it is so successful that fans will clamour for another one. That second one will be called 'The Farewell Tour'. But of course, it won't be. As they say in show business, it will run and run.

However, as the Colonel has foreseen, problems arise with the running order of the show, so he gets Bubba to bring in some bottles of bourbon and scotch to help oil the wheels.

There are so many imponderables to try and resolve. Should the show begin or end with all four of them performing on stage together, like in the famous photograph taken in the Sun studio? In what order should they appear individually? Should Elvis, as the biggest star, go on last or should he open the show? What nobody is saying, but what they are all thinking, is that nobody wants to follow Jerry Lee Lewis. He is utterly unpredictable. Depending on what sort of mood he is in, he can come out and sing a few Hank Williams' songs, or on the other hand, he's been known to set fire to his piano while singing 'Great Balls of Fire'. And how do you top that if you're on next? With no resolution in sight and the liquor almost gone, it is decided to leave any decisions for another meeting in a week's time.

Elvis is determined that he will put on an act as the climax to the show that will outshine Jerry Lee Lewis and the others and confirm that he is the one and only King of Rock and Roll. It will be unbeatable, it will be history-making, it will be talked about for years to come. It will be so good that after the opening night, Jerry Lee will walk on stage at all subsequent shows waving a white flag. And Elvis wants the new act to be running like clockwork by the time of the next meeting of the four of them at Graceland.

"I'm going for something so spectacular that it will shock my fans and take their breath away," Elvis announces at the first rehearsal. Everyone is there: all the members of the TCB Band, his backing singers J D Sumner and the Stamps, the Sweet Inspirations, as well as Colonel Parker, Bubba, Charlie Hodge, his hairdresser Larry Geller and other members of the Memphis Mafia. The hall is so full for this first run-through of Elvis's new closing act that Bubba thinks they should bring in crowd control stewards. Colonel Parker, only half-jokingly, suggests they should have put in turnstiles and charged for admission.

Once people have settled down, he coughs and says "Ahem, Elvis. Pardon me for saying this. I know I take care of business and leave all the music stuff to you. But if I can point out that your fans love the familiarity of your shows, right from the opening numbers to the finish with 'Can't Help Falling In Love With You'. Sure, some of the songs and routines may vary, but what all the fans come to watch time after time is something that has become a great American Institution – an Elvis Presley Show. It works, Elvis. You don't need to try and fix it."

But Elvis insists that the tour must be a catalyst for change. "We're gonna break the mould."

He urges everyone to gather around while he outlines his plans. For the closing act, he will come on wearing a new all-white jumpsuit, specially made for him by Bernard Lansky, with a big gold crown on the chest and the words 'The King.' And like royalty, his cape will be edged with ermine. But there will be one important change to his outfit.

"There's a singer over in England who wears this tall hat covered with small round mirrors. Bernard has made one just like it for me. It will look great in the spotlights like the sun is blazing away on top of my head."

Larry Geller bursts into tears when he hears this. "All the work I've done over the years, Elvis, looking after your hair. Every single day. It's my life's work. And you're gonna go on stage with your hair squashed flat under a hat."

As a kindly gesture, Colonel Parker takes a dingy-looking handkerchief from the sleeve of his jacket and hands it to Larry who inspects it at arm's length, hands it back, and carries on quietly weeping.

Elvis explains that he wants to repeat '2001: A Space Odyssey' which always opens his shows but this time the TCB Band will follow it with 'Good Rockin' Tonight' – one of his best songs and one that harks back to his time at Sun and the Million Dollar Quartet. It's absolutely the right choice. James Burton, Glen Hardin, and all the other members of the band look at each other nervously but Elvis gives them his killer stare. After 30 seconds, the backing singers will then join in and start singing 'Good Rockin' Tonight'. After he has sung a couple of verses, Jerry Lee Lewis, Carl Perkins, and Johnny Cash will come on stage to sing along with him.

Elvis asks if the stage floor is polished, Charlie Hodge, his oldest friend and gofer, who is still wearing a floral pinafore with the pocket stuffed full of yellow dusters, assures him, "Yes, Elvis, it gleams like a mirror. I've spent hours doing it."

"OK, everybody, let's go for a first run–through," says Elvis.

There is a palpable air of tension and excitement among the performers and spectators, wondering just what will emerge from the wings. The band and the backing singers begin playing 'Good Rockin' Tonight' and then suddenly Elvis bursts from the side of the stage, sliding along on his knees in his new jumpsuit and mirror hat, his arms spread wide, Al Jolson-style. The spotlight operated by Lamar Fike picks out the hat covered with mirrors, turning it into a dazzling sun racing across the stage.

Unfortunately, the slide does not slow down and come to a stop by the mic, as intended; instead, Elvis picks up speed and heads for the wings on the other side of the stage.

"I think Elvis is leaving the building," Bubba tells the Colonel as they look on in horror.

There's a scream and then a crash like a load of scrap metal being dumped into a skip, followed by the sound of breaking glass and a piece of scenery falling across the stage. Elvis staggers out, covered in dust and rubble, looking like a miner who's just finished his shift. The hat of which he is so proud looks as if it has been sat upon by Colonel Parker, with only a few mirrors left hanging on.

Everyone is calling out, "Elvis, are you OK?" They swarm around him like flies around a jar of jelly, dusting him down and examining him for injuries. "Look at his hair," sobs Larry Geller. Not being sure of Elvis's mood, the one thing nobody does is laugh. And nobody wants to be the first to make a comment on what has just happened. There is a nervous group silence while they all wait to see how he is going to react.

Elvis coughs, pats some more dust from his jumpsuit, grins, and says, "Well I thought that went pretty well."

There is an audible sigh of relief and immediately shouts of "sensational", "you were fabulous", "it's the best thing you've ever done" and the like are heard around the rehearsal room, accompanied by smiles and thumbs-up signs.

They crowd around Elvis, patting him on the back in congratulation, causing small clouds of dust to rise up around him.

Once he has stopped coughing, he announces, "Charlie, fix that stage. It's too slippery. And then let's do it again."

As soon as they are back at Graceland, the Colonel, who really likes Elvis's idea, and his assistant, Bubba, are hard at work on new merchandising, telling their suppliers in Bangladesh and Soweto that they are going to need 'Good Rockin' Tonight' badges, stickers and posters for the tour. These will be in addition to items such as the blue suede shoes with batteries in the heel that play the famous opening to the song; long black jackets and stetsons for the Johnny Cash fans; 'Whole Lotta Shaking' snow globes and cigarette lighters with the slogan "Great Balls Of Fire'. As he informs Bubba, Colonel Parker is not worried about merchandise for Elvis. He can flood the stalls at the shows with products from his famous storeroom which he will then charge as if newly made. The tour will be a godsend to shift old stock like the red satin heart-shaped cushions with gold fringes that say 'I Love Elvis', the cheap rings to wear around your neck, and the plastic purses.

Jerry Lee Lewis, meanwhile, has his own ideas as to how the Million Dollar Quartet show should finish. His plan is that all four of them should be on stage singing Carl Perkins' Sun hit 'Matchbox'. As the song finishes Carl will hold up to the audience a large box of matches while Elvis and Johnny Cash squirt lighter fuel over the piano being played by Jerry Lee. Carl will strike a match and set fire to the piano and Jerry Lee will lead them in singing 'Great Balls of Fire'. "Oh Lordy, Lordy," he shouts out loud. "What a way to finish the show. We'll go out in a blaze of glory." It will be worth another $5 million at the very least to the takings – a gold-plated home run.

He is sitting at home at his ranch, sipping bourbon, and the more he thinks about his idea, the better he likes it. He suspects

Elvis has plans for how the show should end, but once he hears about the 'Great Balls Of Fire' idea he'll climb right on board with Ole Jerry Lee. He's so impatient to talk to him about it that he doesn't notice the time as he climbs into his white Lincoln Continental and heads for Graceland. All he knows is that Elvis is going to love it.

He pulls up outside the Music Gates and presses the intercom. "Open up the gates. It's The Killer and I'm here for Elvis."

Minnie Mae is up late in the kitchen skinning a couple of rabbits ready for tomorrow's dinner. She moves to stand next to the intercom and says, "Come agin. Wut's that you'se a-sayin'?"

"I said it's The Killer and I'm here to see Elvis about the Million Dollars Quartet shows."

What with the crackle over the intercom system and her own hearing not being what it was, Minnie Mae thinks that she is dealing with a killer who wants Elvis for a quarter of a million dollars ransom. At least that's what she thinks he is saying.

"No way!" she shouts.

"Now listen up. This is really important and I don't want to stand around here wasting any more time. I want to see Elvis. So open up them gates or I do declare I'll get mad enough to shoot my way through."

"Mister Killer, ah got mah Granpappy Hood's ole buffalo gun here with me. Yer need ter be afeared."

"Ha ha ha. I'm laughing fit to be hog-tied. Why it's the middle of the night and I reckon you'd be hard pushed to hit the side of a barn."

"Ah'm a-warnin' yer. Ah'm a-wearin' mah night vision goggles, Mister Killer."

Jerry Lee Lewis walks back to his car, takes out his Derringer pistol from the glove compartment, and starts shooting at the Music Gates. The lock flies off, he pushes the gates open and walks back to his car, and then...

Boom! Suddenly the whole front of Jerry Lee's Lincoln Continental explodes and disintegrates into a heap of small chunks of smoking metal.

"What the..." he shouts and flings himself behind the wall of the grounds. He looks at the pistol in his hand and then the wreckage of his car. It is like he is up against a tank when he is armed with a peashooter. He crawls back to his car, snaps off the aerial, ties a white handkerchief to it, and then waves it above the wall.

With blue lights flashing and sirens wailing, the police arrive just as another shot from Minnie Mae smashes into Jerry Lee's car. All that is now recognisable of the Lincoln Continental is the boot and the two back wheels. The rest is reduced to rubble.

"Hi Jerry Lee, I see it's you again," says the officer in charge. "What've you done – declared war on Graceland?"

"Get the National Guard," he tells them. "You boys are out-gunned."

As far as the police can tell, what seems to have happened is that Jerry Lee turned up at the wrong time in the middle of the night; Minnie Mae couldn't hear properly what he was saying and thought someone wanted to kill Elvis.

It all added up to one big mistake that resulted in them both being involved in a shoot-out, being arrested, and put in adjoining cells at the police station.

While still in the cells, Minnie Mae insists to Elvis, Colonel Parker, and the Chief of Police, "All ah knows is that ah thought ah wus a-protectin' the boy from a killer. An that's the truth, Ah ain't lookin' fer no favours. Ah can do mah time." But the Police Chief is so keen to see her leave he practically carries her outside. The mugshots that were taken of her that make her look like an elderly Bonnie Parker, are quietly given to her along with her fingerprints, the Police Chief being anxious to remove all trace of her short stay in the cells. Minnie Mae looks admiringly at the photographs, each with a number underneath. "Lookee Elvis, they be a nice selection o' pictures o' me. Would yer like me ter git one framed fer Graceland?"

Meanwhile, Jerry Lee Lewis is driving back to his ranch in a brand new white Lincoln Continental, bought for him by Elvis to replace the one blasted into smithereens by Minne Mae. "Once again Ole Jerry Lee has beaten the rap," he says to himself, conveniently forgetting Elvis and the Colonel's influence in securing his release. He quotes a short passage from the Bible to himself, "When hard pressed, I cried to the Lord; he brought me into a spacious place." That is what he believes: that the Good Lord always takes care of Jerry Lee.

That night, he remembers he has still not talked to Elvis about his ideas for closing the Million Dollar Quartet shows, and although it is late, he decides to get into his car and head for Graceland. But as bad luck would have it, when he gets there, he finds that Elvis is fast asleep and Minnie Mae is once again working in the kitchen and answering the intercom as he demands to be let inside to see Elvis.

Ends

6. The Forgotten Wedding Anniversary

"Elvis, honey, do you happen to know what day it is tomorrow?" asks Priscilla, trying to look winsome, while fluttering her mascara-weighted false eyelashes like the flaps on a jet aeroplane.

"Wow, that's a tough one," replies Elvis, thoughtfully stroking his chin. "I think I ought to ask Charlie just to be sure. He's good at that sort of thing."

"Now think really hard, Elvis. It's important."

There is a long silence before he announces, looking so pleased with himself, "I've got it! It's Tuesday!"

"No, no, no, no, no no," shouts Priscilla who, in her fury, stamps her foot so hard that she punches a hole in the carpet of the Jungle Room with the Eiffel Tower-tall stiletto of her shoe. "No Mr. Fool. It's our wedding anniversary! And I do declare, you've plumb forgotten it! How could you!"

Elvis begins to fiddle with the fringe of his jumpsuit, all the while wondering where is Colonel Parker, his manager, when you need him most. What worries him is that he is going to have to think fast and rely on his own imagination to come up with something convincing, and that's always a risky strategy.

"Why Satnin' (his pet name for Priscilla, and always a good card to play at times like this) of course I know that. It's burned on my heart. I've got a very special present for you and I've asked Minnie Mae to cook up something fancy for our anniversary dinner."

Priscilla does not look as impressed as he hoped. "Elvis, I'm going to say this just once. There is absolutely no way that we are going to have Minnie Mae's chitlins or raccoon fricassee on our wedding anniversary. And I don't want a home delivery meal deal from the Piggly Wiggly supermarket either. We're going to go somewhere special and have a romantic dinner for two. Am I making myself crystal clear? Somewhere with class. So get it fixed."

She glares at him and then stalks off, 5 feet 4 inches of indignation. Or 5 feet 11 inches if you count to the top of her lacquered bouffant hair, and also take into account her stilettos.

"Colonel, sir, I have to report a serious dereliction of duty in the management of my affairs," reports Elvis. "And I am mighty disappointed in the way I've been let down."

His manager takes a couple of puffs of his cigar while he concocts a reply. "Well, son," he begins, "I'm in the process of concluding a $1.25 million contract for you to appear in Hal Wallis's next picture. A movie he reckons he can finish shooting in 12 days. Now if you don't mind my saying, that's nice work and it doesn't sound like I'm failing you."

"Yea, I'm sure it will do wonders for my career," says Elvis, injecting an unusual level of sarcasm into his response. "But the point is you forgot to remind me that it's our wedding anniversary tomorrow. It made me look bad in front of Priscilla when she asked me about it."

The Colonel decides to go for a sorrowful expression combined with a slow shake of his head, downcast eyes, and a noisy blowing of his nose. "I've been working so hard taking care of business, son. I haven't had time to step off the treadmill. But Bubba will show you the diary where it's written that it's the very next thing I was going to do. Isn't that right, Bubba?"

His assistant opens the diary and turns to the page which, as he suspects, is blank apart from a meeting with a slot machine manufacturer that evening. He opts for nodding his head, which can mean anything. Elvis explains that Priscilla is expecting a romantic dinner for two at a classy restaurant, and then there's the present and the card to sort out. There is not a lot of time left, so he is going to need help to get things organised. Or life for him, and by extension, everybody else in Graceland, will be hell.

"We certainly don't want the Tiny Terror on the warpath," grumbles the Colonel.

He wafts his cigar, while saying a silent prayer, and guarantees delivery of their best ever wedding anniversary.

Once Elvis has left the office, Bubba, the Colonel's assistant, says that they have let him down. "We should have known about the wedding anniversary, kept a record of it somewhere, and told him in good time."

Within the privacy of his office, the Colonel is prepared to admit that he may well be correct and that they should now do all they can to put things right. He tells Bubba to book the Pasta Its Best restaurant and to call Bernard Lansky and ask him to come and see him at once so that he can make a suitable outfit for Elvis for the big night.

But after making some calls his assistant informs him that Pasta Its Best is no longer what it was, so he has booked another Italian restaurant near the Peabody Hotel.

Colonel Parker decides to take a look in the storeroom where he keeps all his Elvis merchandise – hallowed ground where no one else is allowed to enter – to see if there is anything suitable for Elvis to give his wife. He greets them as affectionately as if they were his children, patting the red satin cushions trimmed with gold fringes, lightly dusting the rings and necklaces with a flick of his handkerchief, arranging the cowboy hats into tidy stacks, and doing a quick visual stocktake. He looks on at all the merchandise accumulated there with the reverence of an art expert gazing on a newly discovered Caravaggio painting.

After some minutes of searching, he strikes gold – a card with a colour shot from the 'Blue Hawaii' movie which, when you open it, plays 'Hawaiian Wedding Song'. "Perfect," he smiles to himself as he returns to his desk. "It's a start."

Elvis goes to see his grandmother, Minnie Mae, in the kitchen to explain that he and Priscilla are going out to some fancy restaurant to celebrate their wedding anniversary. He feels bad and wants to apologise because he knows that she will be cooking something special, probably not to Priscilla's taste but you can bet it will be one of his favourites.

"Don't pay it no mind, son," she shrugs. "Ah knows Priscilla dun set her heart on goin' out an' a-doin' somethin' different, somethin' more classy. Ah surely do understand. But there'll be a real treat a-waitin' fer you when you git back."

He wonders what treat he has to look forward to.

"Ah asked mah cousin, Cain Hood, ter send down a possum," she tells him. "Cooked in a pie, with a pastry top an' dumplings, it'll remind yer of the old days in Tupelo."

"But Dodger (a name he sometimes calls her), he can't be sending dead possums in the post. It must be against the law."

Minnie Mae titters and tells him that it was sent live in a cage and she'll kill it and skin it later. She is also planning to pickle some hogs trotters, another of his favourites.

"Anyways, ah'm sure there'll be a-plenty left fer the rest of the family ter enjoy the fine dinin'," she calls out as Colonel Parker walks into the kitchen.

"Why, I'd like to make a reservation right now," he responds, crossing his fingers behind his back and thinking very hard where else he can be at the time.

"Elvis, can we have a word about what's happening tomorrow?"

Elvis believes that something spectacular is needed as a present for Priscilla to redeem the situation, and he has an idea that he outlines to his manager who, the more he hears, the more the colour drains from his face.

"Colonel, sir, I know it is a tough assignment, but if anybody can do it, then you can. Do whatever it takes to make it happen."

"I won't be pulling strings, son. I'll be giving them one helluva yank," he tells Elvis.

That evening, on the day of the wedding anniversary, Charlie Hodge, his gofer, drives Elvis and Priscilla to drop them off at the Mamma Mia Here We Eat Again Italian restaurant in Peabody Place where they are greeted by Mamma Mia herself; she shows them to a table discreetly situated in a corner.

Elvis is wearing the special jumpsuit made for him overnight by Bernard Lansky: it is in white leather, with flared trousers, a high stiff collar, and a cape. On the chest is a big gold-coloured number 5 (it's their fifth wedding anniversary) and five candles which, when a hidden switch is pressed, light up. The belt buckle comprises two interlocking gold rings.

Priscilla, who is wearing a black Holly Golightly-style dress made for her by Hollywood designer Edith Head, is instantly captivated by the restaurant. The tables have red and white checked cloths, there are candles stuck in chianti bottles and the menu is written in chalk on a blackboard on the wall.

"Oh Elvis, thank you so much," she enthuses. "What a great idea to come here. I love it. It's like we've stepped into a restaurant in Italy. It's so authentic. And by the way, honey, I think you can switch off those lights on your jumpsuit. They're fun but they're getting to be a bit of a distraction."

When Priscilla has finished her sea bass and green salad main course, Elvis presents her with the 'Blue Hawaii' card found for him by Colonel Parker and a small gift-wrapped box about the size of a cigarette packet.

"Happy wedding anniversary, Satnin'," he tells her.

What with the tacky card and the smallness of the gift she finds it very difficult to hide her disappointment. But she manages a weak smile and a curt thank-you. She gives a shake to the box which makes a rattling noise, leading her to suspect she is about to find some dreadful piece of yellow metal costume jewellery saying 'I Luv Elvis' that has come from the Colonel's storeroom. If Elvis really did forget their anniversary, it is probably all the two of them have managed to cobble together in the past 24 hours. If he starts to sing 'Won't you wear my ring around your neck' I'll kill him, she thinks. Curiously, however, Elvis is smiling and does not seem at all nervous about how she will react to the present he has given her.

"What?" she exclaims as she opens the box to reveal a set of car keys. "Oh wow. You've got me a car."

"Close your eyes and come with me," says Elvis, taking her by the hand and leading her outside. She is desperately hoping that the car is not something that Colonel Parker has bought at an auction.

But no, when she opens her eyes, there, parked next to the sidewalk, is a Ford Mustang. But it is not any Ford Mustang, he tells her. It is the one driven by Steve McQueen in the movie 'Bullitt' and it is hers for the next two weeks until her own model is delivered to Graceland.

Priscilla screams with delight and leaps to hug Elvis, causing him to wince as her heavily lacquered bouffant hair collides with his face. She walks slowly around the car, running a finger along the bodywork, before getting inside and sitting behind the wheel.

"You can drive us home later, honey," he tells her. "And oh, I nearly forgot. I've booked us a holiday in San Francisco so you can drive around the same streets that Steve McQueen does in the movie."

She lets out another scream of joy, flings herself at Elvis who sustains another blow to the face from her hairdo.

They are nearing the end of the meal, having a coffee and finishing the bottle of wine, when Colonel Parker walks in carrying a bouquet of flowers which he presents to Priscilla and wishes them both a happy wedding anniversary.

"It's from everybody at Graceland," he tells her. "We all chipped in to buy it."

From the look of the flowers and the cellophane wrapping and the faint whiff of diesel fumes she guesses it has come from a gas station, probably in the last five minutes. Did he really use all the money to buy this bunch of flowers, she thinks to herself?

"Are you joining us, Colonel Parker, sir?" says Elvis.

He smiles benignly and replies that he simply wants to make sure everything is going well on their special wedding anniversary night out. He doffs his faded yellow straw trilby, nods to them both in turn, and heads off towards the kitchen.

He tells Mamma Mia not to bother Elvis with the bill but to send it directly to him. He and Priscilla have loved their visit to the restaurant and, on their behalf, by way of saying thank you, he would like to present her with a framed certificate to hang in the restaurant. It declares in an ornate Gothic typeface, 'Elvis was here and he loved it'. There is also a big splodge of a red seal at the bottom of the certificate.

Mama Mia is so thrilled that she hugs the certificate tightly to her chest and confides that tonight she will sleep with it under her pillow. "Grazie, Godfather," she says, and attempts to kiss the Colonel's hand.

"Oh no, Mrs. Mama Mia," he answers, becoming flustered. "I'm Elvis's manager and I'm here to make sure everything is just right for their wedding anniversary. I'm no Godfather." He shakes his head vigorously to emphasize his denial.

Mama Mia turns to the rest of her family in the kitchen and says, "Omerta." She winks, raises a finger to her lips, and adds, "Don Colonel – issa da big shush, OK. We no say a word."

"Now about the bill for the meal…"

She rips it up into several pieces and flings them to the floor. She insists, "For Elvis, issa no charge. Issa gift."

It is exactly the reaction Colonel Parker was hoping for on what is a test run. Mamma Mia is the first establishment to receive such an Elvis certificate – but the way things have gone, it won't be the last. A couple of dozen others have been printed and framed – unknown to Elvis, naturally – so that he can repeat this wheeze again and again at other places like restaurants and hotels, and hopefully, get the same result as tonight. The message 'Elvis was here and loved it' is a very powerful endorsement, but the one flaw is that it does omit the name of the establishment. But, he reasons, it will probably be overlooked in all the excitement of the Elvis name and the signature which the Colonel himself has carefully signed at the bottom. It is a scheme, he tells his assistant, Bubba, that he has borrowed from the Queen of England who lets places where she likes to eat and shop put up a coat of arms saying 'By Royal Appointment'.

"Nobody, Bubba, and I repeat nobody, has ever seen her open up her purse and pay for anything. Ever. On her way out, one of her retainers hands over a plaque and away she goes. If it works for her, it will work for Elvis."

A week later the phone rings in the Colonel's office. He picks up and hears a voice saying, "Issa dat Don Colonel? Dis issa Don Giovanni here. My respects because I hear lots offa good things about you, Don Colonel, from our people in Memphis. They like-a how you take care offa da business."

"No, no, no, you've got it all wrong," he protests. "I'm Colonel Parker, not Don Colonel. He must be somebody else."

"Do notta worry, Don Colonel. Your secret issa safe with me."

Ends

Elvis on tour in 1972

Elvis with Colonel Tom Parker, who officially became his manager in March 1956

The Jungle Room at Graceland where Elvis used to hang out with the Memphis Mafia

Elvis and Priscilla on their wedding day on May 1 1967 in Las Vegas

Hal Wallis (left) produced many of Elvis's films, including 'King Creole' and 'GI Blues'. He joins Elvis and Shirley MacLaine to celebrate Dean Martin's birthday

Liberace's Las Vegas shows, like those of Elvis's, were hugely successful

Elvis with his father Vernon

Charlie Hodge, Elvis's devoted friend, hands him a towel during rehearsals. He first met Elvis in 1956

7. The Fall and Rise of Rex Rabbit

Bubba opens the door to Colonel Parker's office at Graceland and reels back in shock at what he sees. It is a sight that is simply beyond belief, as if he has suddenly stepped into the realms of fantasy. He could not have had a bigger shock if he had sat down briefly on Old Sparky, and he needs to lean for support against the wall in the corridor to try and recover his senses. Can he really have seen that? Should he be questioning his own sanity?

He opens the door a fraction to take a peek and confirm what he saw and yes, he was right. Although it is midday, or the middle of the night for Elvis, whose time clock is the reverse of everyone else's at Graceland, Bubba decides he needs to go and wake him up immediately. Elvis is stunned by the news and they go to seek the advice of Dr. Nick about what may have happened to his manager.

"Are you qualified to treat mental health issues or problems relating to the mind?" Elvis asks his personal physician. Dr. Nick sets aside his lunch of stuffed vine leaves and olives, pausing only to pop a clove of garlic into his mouth, before getting up and moving over to the wall of his office-cum-consulting-room-cum-dispensary to study the array of framed certificates that hang there. He moves along slowly, looking at each one in turn, before finally tapping one with his finger.

"I thought so. There it is," he tells them. The certificate from the University of Swampwater, with its elaborate coat of arms and big red wax seal, confirms that Dr. Nick has completed the three-month $500 correspondence course and is now a fully qualified psychologist, psychoanalyst, and psychiatrist.

"Excellent. Colonel Parker will be in the safest possible hands," says a relieved Elvis.

Dr. Nick puts a notepad into his mobile dispensary – a suitcase on wheels with a big red cross – and a selection of enemas.

Constipation is his particular field of expertise and, as he explains to them, it is a complaint that can have unpredictable side effects on the mind. "We need to be prepared for all eventualities", he cautions.

Once the thick clouds of cigar smoke begin to disperse the three of them can see Colonel Parker sitting behind his desk. Instead of his usual yellow straw trilby, a large set of rabbit ears is perched on top of his head. What is more, he seems entirely unconcerned as he goes about his business of sifting through a pile of invoices, most of which end up in the wastepaper bin.

"Colonel, sir, are you feeling all right?" asks Elvis, an edge of panic in his voice. "You don't seem yourself if you don't mind my mentioning it."

Dr. Nick decides to take charge and walks forward and, after eventually remembering that it is located in his wrist, he takes the Colonel's pulse.

"Have you been having any bad dreams about foxes or weasels? Is something worrying you? You can tell me, I'm a doctor. And by the way, is everything all right down there?" He points a finger towards the huge wobbly mound that is the Colonel's stomach. "No constipation?"

"Let me speak plainly, Colonel, sir," declares Elvis. "We're mighty concerned as to why you're wearing rabbit ears. Of course, it can be your secret, but have you joined the Playboy Club for instance?"

The Colonel indicates that he is fine. "Take a seat fellers and let me explain. I've been to see Rex Rabbit and I've seen the future."

He tells them of a visit he made to California to the Bunnyland amusement park. He was invited to meet the CEO, Bunny Warren Junior, and other members of the board to offer some advice on how they can make more money out of the business, and also investigate possible joint projects between Elvis and the Bunnyland Corporation. He'll talk about these later at dinner when everyone is there.

"I reckon things went well because we've had an invitation to go back for another meeting, and this time I'm to bring Elvis and his family," he reports.

"And this arrived today," he adds pointing to a sleek-looking gaming machine beside his desk; the others note that the old model, which the Colonel has used for years, has been pushed back into a corner.

"It's all electric," explains Colonel Parker. "I just have to push a button, so there's no strain on my arms and shoulders. No Repetitive Injury Strain worries. No pain, all gain. I'm impressed. They tell me that when I win – and I must admit I haven't yet – three faces of Rex Rabbit will pop up. And by the way, here's the letter that came with it."

He hands it over to Elvis to read.

From Bunny Warren Jnr
CEO
Bunnyland Corporation
California

Dear Colonel Tom Parker
Thank you so much for your insights into how we can make major improvements to the profitability of our business here at Bunnyland. Your premise is that it does not really matter who is dressed up as Rex Rabbit because who can tell, and therefore employing people to wear a costume for one dollar an hour and all the carrots they can eat was certainly thought-provoking. We decided we would try it out and got a lot of applications, but unfortunately most seemed to come from vagrants. A couple of applicants were given the job on a trial basis but we had to let them go because they were making a nuisance of themselves, pestering adults and children alike for money and cigarettes.
Visitors – or our guests, as we like to call them – were very upset because it is not the sort of behaviour they expect from our beloved Rex Rabbit. In one instance, a fight broke out that resulted in a guest, who would not hand over a cigarette, being floored by a punch from Rex Rabbit. Children, in particular, were very distressed to see him being led away in handcuffs by the police.

On reflection, the board feels it is worth putting up with the costs of paying more for the right sort of people to represent our popular walk-around characters like Rex Rabbit and Hurry Hare.

As regards our merchandise, your expertise in this field is second to none, so thank you for your recommendations of certain workshops in Bangladesh and Soweto in South Africa. I'm sure they do sterling work for you and Elvis but I feel we would need to inspect these establishments before agreeing to any contracts with them. Hopefully, we can then also negotiate the terms of your commission.

Your idea of a movie featuring Elvis and Rex Rabbit is certainly an exciting one, but I must point out that Rex does not do rock and roll, at least not yet!

Please arrange another visit to see us and we can talk some more about this project and, at the same time, our ideas on how you can develop brand new and highly profitable lines of entertainment on behalf of Elvis.

Please extend this invitation to Elvis and his family whom we would be delighted to welcome to Bunnyland. I know they will be given a '24-carrot' reception!

Yours in entertainment

Bunny Warren Jnr.

Colonel Parker asks them if they believe in fate. Elvis, Bubba, and Dr. Nick look blankly at each other and shrug their shoulders, wondering what on earth he is talking about. He tells them that it was in the stars that two of the biggest entertainment organisations in the world, Elvis and the Bunnyland Corporation, would one day work together. He points out that the day he took over as Elvis's manager was the same day that Bunnyland first opened its gates to visitors. They began their journeys at the same time and now their paths have intersected.

"It's Serengeti. I think that's the word," he adds.

He lights a new cigar and pushes a button on his new gaming machine which whirrs quietly for a few seconds before popping up with three sad-faced Hurry Hares, their mouths downturned in regret. He loses.

"Remember to get me a screwdriver later, will you, Bubba. It probably just needs a couple of tweaks."

At dinner, Colonel Parker reminds them of the invitation for Elvis and his family, which, he presumes, means his wife Priscilla and their daughter, Lisa Marie, to accompany him on his next visit to Bunnyland. It is certain to attract tremendous publicity, not least because he has already alerted the media and he suspects that Bunnyland will have done the same. It is a perfect win–win for both parties.

In that case, says Priscilla, it is absolutely vital that they all look their best for the cameras. She will invite Edith Head, the top Hollywood costume designer, to come to Graceland to make some outfits for herself and Lisa Marie, while Elvis adds that he will arrange for Bernard Lansky to design an appropriate jumpsuit for him to wear.

But just when the Colonel is about to move on to the next item of business, Vernon, Elvis's father, raises his hand and says he is family and he would like to go to Bunnyland as well. It is somewhere he has never been – like Coney Island – and he'd love to go. Then up go the hands of Minnie Mae, Elvis's grandmother, and Aunt Delta, who don't want to miss out on the fun.

The Colonel begins to fret, worried about the escalating costs, and he starts scribbling a lot of numbers on his paper napkin. But Elvis insists that, since they are family, they should all go.

However, the size of the entourage continues to get ever larger with the addition of Charlie Hodge, Elvis's chief gofer and cheerleader, Dr. Nick, his personal physician, and his hairdresser Larry Geller. More paper napkins are used, and more figures are scribbled down and crossed out as the Colonel becomes increasingly exasperated as the numbers and the costs climb remorselessly higher and higher.

Then Red and Sonny West are added in case there are any security issues.

Finally, the Colonel can stand it no longer and he bursts like a balloon.

"Security? What's going to happen? Are we going to be attacked by a gang of rabbits? I don't think so!"

His face is watermelon-red as he adds, "Bunnyland will think they are being invaded when we all turn up. They'll make a dash for the bunkers."

"More likely it will be rabbit holes," smirks Charlie. There is a very frosty silence in response to his joke, so he concentrates on making himself as small as possible and folding his yellow duster to be ready to resume his household chores.

Finally, it is decided that with so many of them going, they need to hire a luxury coach, which means Lamar Fike, another member of the Memphis Mafia, is added to the headcount as the driver.

But there is a major crisis before the coach even sets off down the drive towards the Music Gates when Elvis emerges onto the portico of the house, proudly posing in his new specially made jumpsuit. "What do you think"? he asks them all. "I bet they're gonna love this outfit at Bunnyland."

Emblazoned on the chest of his all-white jumpsuit, with its high stiff collar and flared trousers, is a large picture of Bugs Bunny; there is also an image of Foghorn Leghorn on the cape, while a large round belt buckle proclaims 'That's all folks!'

His smile quickly fades when he notices the looks of horror, the heartfelt sighs, and the shaking of heads from everybody else. He is surrounded by a circle of anguish.

"Oh Elvis! How could you!" yells Priscilla. "They'll never let us into Bunnyland with you looking like that." She turns to her daughter and says, "Lisa Marie, will you please explain to Daddy what's wrong."

"You see, Daddy, what you're wearing are Warner Brothers cartoon characters – not Bunnyland ones. Every kid knows that Bugs Bunny and Rex Rabbit are deadly enemies."

"Turning up in that outfit, honey, will be the worst kind of insult," declares Priscilla. "It's akin to spitting on Bunny Warren Senior's grave."

"Oh no," groans Elvis. "What am I gonna do?"

The solution is to send for Bernard Lansky so that he can make some running repairs to the outfit during the journey and yet another person is added to the headcount. The Colonel points out that with so many of them now heading for Bunnyland, he needs his assistant, Bubba, to be included in the party.

The Colonel's misery is complete when Elvis points out that the entire household of Graceland, with the exception of Old Shep the dog, is now heading for Bunnyland.

During the journey, Colonel Parker takes the opportunity to talk to Elvis about some of the ideas he discussed with the Bunnyland Corporation on his previous visit, plus some of his own concerning the establishment of an Elvis Presley theme park.

When Elvis looks bemused by the notion, he tells him when they get there to look carefully at what has been done at the amusement park, and then imagine what it could be like if it was all about him instead of Rex Rabbit and his furry pals.

He urges him to study all the attractions when they tour the site and see how they can use it as a blueprint to do it even better at an Elvis Presley theme park. For instance, they can have a Heartbreak Hotel for visitors, a stage for shows, a 'Love Me Tender' wedding chapel, attractions like a 'Mystery Train' ghost ride, a Minnie Mae down home style restaurant, and, of course, lots of stalls selling Elvis merchandise.

"Bunnyland say we'd also need our own version of a walk-around Rex Rabbit character," continues Colonel Parker. "So I'm thinking of someone who will dress up in the costume of a big cuddly dog called Old Shep, and I reckon it is just the job for Charlie Hodge," he sniggers.

"He'd have lots of fun chasing after balls thrown by the kids, rolling over to have his tummy tickled, and holding out a paw to shake hands. Of course, we might have to source a steady supply of fleas, just to keep it authentic." It is a prospect he plainly finds hilarious as part of his ongoing feud with Charlie.

"This theme park wouldn't be built at Graceland, would it?" asks Elvis nervously, already imagining Priscilla's reaction.

"No, son, we'd need a much, much bigger site. Maybe somewhere out Tupelo way would be ideal. Then we can incorporate the cabin where you were born as part of the theme park.

"Bunnyland say what with your popularity as the King of Rock and Roll and one of Hollywood's top film stars, it will be a gold mine. You have millions of fans around the world and, believe me, they will all want to come. And they'll be thinking to themselves they might just bump into Elvis himself while they're walking around your theme park."

"They're more likely to meet Charlie dressed up as Old Shep," remarks Elvis.

Colonel Parker is keen to put some distance between any possible new Elvis theme park and what Bunnyland does. He believes that they attract mainly kids who spend their money on bubblegum and Rex Rabbit big ears hats. But Elvis's fans are that much older and have much bigger spending power.

And for his really old fans they could also establish a 'Happy Days Are Here Again' retirement home on part of the site.

Elvis is aghast at the idea of an old people's home being part of the theme park.

But the Colonel explains that these sort of developments make a lot of money because, after all, what do the residents do all day? They mainly sleep and they don't eat a lot, activities that don't cost a lot of money. And anyway, it can be located in a distant corner of the park.

"Elvis, son, this whole theme park project can be bigger than Texas, as they say. It'll be like a whole community, or maybe even like a town, with all the facilities you'd find there. It can be so big that I'm betting that the Bunnyland Corporation will be itching to buy in and get a piece of the action. Your theme park can end up making Bunnyland look like a kindergarten."

Elvis starts to laugh and places a hand on the Colonel's shoulder and wags a finger at him. "And tell me, just by any chance, amongst all these fantastic plans of yours, will there be a casino at this theme park of mine?"

The Colonel tries on his astonished expression, eyes and mouth open wide, and he even manages to retain it for a few seconds.

He shakes his head in wonderment. "Do you know, son, I hadn't thought of that. It is certainly worth thinking about..."

"I bet it is," Elvis tells him, still laughing.

Bunnyland CEO, Bunny Warren Junior, and the rest of the welcoming party watch as more and more people follow Elvis in getting off the coach.

"Wow! I didn't realise you had such a big family, Elvis," comments the CEO. He is accompanied by an identikit collection of executives in their Brooks Brothers suits, white button-down shirts, and crew cut hairstyles.

The visit has attracted huge crowds of spectators and barriers have been erected with security guards posted every few yards, but the fans press forward to get a better glimpse of Elvis, and the guards are struggling to keep the barriers upright and hold the crowds at bay. "Elvis! Elvis! We love Elvis!" most of them are chanting.

Bernard Lansky has done a great job in making alterations to Elvis's jumpsuit and Rex Rabbit twitches his nose and whiskers and claps his hands with delight on seeing an image of himself on the chest of Elvis's jumpsuit. (The illustration of Foghorn Leghorn on the cape has been replaced by one of Hurry Hare.)

Everyone begins to shuffle together to line up for the photographs, with Elvis and Rex Rabbit in the centre, flanked on either side by Colonel Parker and Bunny Warren Junior.

"This is a historic day when the two greatest entertainers in the world meet – Elvis and Rex Rabbit," announces the CEO. "I am proud and delighted on behalf of the Bunnyland organisation to welcome Elvis and his family here today. Clearly, all the fans are happy too, with so many of them having come to witness this occasion. On such a special day it is only right that our founder, Bunny Warren Senior, should be here as well."

Elvis looks puzzled and whispers, "Pardon me, sir, but I thought he was dead."

Bunny Warren Junior points to a table draped with a black velvet cloth on which stands a small Grecian-style urn. "Oh he's here all right," he adds.

Dozens of bulbs pop like a starburst of Roman candles as the photographers start taking pictures of the group. The hordes of fans continue to press forward, still calling out "Elvis! Elvis! We love you!" Suddenly the barriers buckle and collapse and the fans surge forward like a tidal wave, surrounding Elvis, while Rex Rabbit is knocked to the ground. Others in the photo shoot are borne away by the stampede, like flotsam on a flood tide, and Rex Rabbit is left dazed in a dusty heap on the ground, one ear almost ripped off and his cos lettuce tie skew whiff under the remaining ear.

He sits there like a battlefield casualty, trying to make sense of what is happening because Bunnyland doesn't do roughhouse riots; it is way beyond the cutesy, genteel behaviour that is part of his daily routine of waves, handshakes, and cuddles.

Any thoughts of going to help him are abandoned immediately when the CEO and the other executives notice that the table on which the urn was standing has been knocked over; horrified, they scramble on the floor to scoop up what they can of Bunny Warren Senior's ashes and put as much of them as they can back into the urn.

Some yards away, Elvis pleads with the mob of fans that surround him that he'll sing a few songs and sign autographs and have his picture taken with them as soon as everybody calms down.

Noticing Rex Rabbit's distress and that no one has gone to his assistance, Aunt Delta hands him her hip flask and tells him, "Here Mr. Rabbit, y'all take a few big slugs of this an' ah surely do swear it'll make you feel a whole sight better. Y'all be as right as rain in next to no time."

Believing it to be some form of medicine, he follows her advice and takes several large glugs. In seconds, the passage between his throat and his stomach is a trail of fire. Poor Rex Rabbit slumps back down, clutching his throat, convinced he has just swallowed napalm. In fact, there is not a lot of difference, because what he has consumed is a large draught of Aunt Delta's homemade hooch, which is nearly pure alcohol since she always likes a drink with a bit of a kick.

Unlike her mother, Minnie Mae, she was never one for baking cakes or making bread; when she was young, nearly all her efforts ended up being given to the hogs. But even then her bakes had to be disguised in the swill because if the word got out that they were being given anything cooked by Delta the hogs would scatter to the far corners of the field. But she knew how to operate an illegal moonshine still by the time she was in junior high school. Give her some potato peelings and molasses and she was a whizz. Folks in Tupelo used to say: 'Don't stand too close to a naked flame if you've been drinking young Delta's hooch or your breath might just catch fire'.

Rex Rabbit totters to his feet, his brain spinning round in his head like a whirligig. As he reels about he grabs at people to stop himself from falling over again, and he is vaguely aware of hearing shrieks and a woman shouting, "take your hands off me."

Elvis is allowed to visit him in the cells at the police station where he finds him sitting on a steel bench, his head bowed and one ear still hanging loose.

"I guess it was a bad day," says Elvis, putting a consoling hand on his shoulder.

"I've seen your Rap Sheet, Rex old buddy, and it doesn't look too good. They're thinking of charging you with being drunk and disorderly and there are those two charges hanging over you from another incident for begging with threatening behaviour and assault."

Elvis has persuaded the Bunnyland Corporation to keep the situation hush-hush and to delay sending in their big-hitter lawyers for the time being. He's promised to be discreet and to try and get Rex Rabbit out without a stain on his character.

"They're making me out to be some kind of a hoodlum, and I'm not. I'm an entertainer. I swear I'm innocent. I'm squeaky clean."

He explains that he thought he was being given medicine to revive him after being knocked down in the crush. How was he to know he was drinking some kind of lethal hooch. Elvis nods his head knowingly. His Aunt Delta drinks it as if it were soda pop.

And as for the other charges, they are down to another Rex Rabbit.

"You mean there's more than one of you?" queries Elvis, clearly surprised by this news.

"Oh yeah. You've seen mice in cages spinning round in a treadmill, haven't you? Well, it's much the same for all of us Rex Rabbits. There's a squad of us because there always has to be at least one on duty around the clock."

He explains that the job does not just involve hopping around the amusement park and saying 'Hi' to the guests. Rex Rabbit also has to visit schools and hospitals, attend charity and corporate events, do film premieres and TV shows. Just one Rex Rabbit could never cope with the workload and he admits he has probably forgotten more duties than he has remembered.

"Don't despair, Rex. Dr. Nick and I are going to see the police captain and sort this out."

"Rex Rabbit drunk and disorderly? How can such a thing be true of one of America's greatest icons?" Elvis insists to the police chief. It is like finding out that George Washington was an inveterate liar and having to rewrite every history book.

"And do you want to be the guy whose face is plastered across every TV station and newspaper throughout the world for falsely arresting him and breaking the hearts of millions of kiddies?" demands Elvis.

"But Elvis, he was as tight as a tick, reeling all over the place, and grabbing at people," insists the police chief.

Dr. Nick coughs by way of an interruption and explains that he is Elvis's personal physician and he has conducted a thorough medical examination of Rex Rabbit. By way of an endorsement of his credentials, he produces a portmanteau that contains upwards of 15 medical qualifications that would cover most departments in a city hospital, including, apparently, gynaecology. The police chief is dazzled.

He says that the truth is that Rex Rabbit had a severe reaction to some medicine that was given to him by a member of the public who thought they were trying to help, but the results turned out to be catastrophic. "He is unwell and needs medical help not gaol time."

"Do you want to be known as the police captain who keeps a very sick Rex Rabbit in a police cell when he should be in a hospital bed?" Elvis asks him again.

"No, Elvis, of course I don't," he admits. "And since it is you who's asking..."

Any trace of a drunk and disorderly charge is erased from the records, as are those relating to begging with menaces and assault which, Elvis reports, were carried out by an imposter trying to blacken the good name of the Bunnyland organisation.

From hereon in, he says, the situation will be handled by his manager, Colonel Parker. Meanwhile, Bernard Lansky is summoned to make sure that Rex Rabbit looks his best when he reappears in public.

He emerges from the police station in a wheelchair pushed by Elvis and attached to a drip held aloft by Dr. Nick. He is greeted with applause from Bunny Warren Junior and a supporting cast of executives.

Elvis tells the TV cameras and reporters that he and Dr. Nick have not left his side for the past 48 hours. It was touch and go after he was given some unknown concoction by a well-meaning member of the public which caused his collapse. He pays tribute to the police captain for making his station available in an emergency when there may not have been time to get Rex to a hospital. There is a round of applause for the police chief who looks suitably grateful.

Rex Rabbit motions to Elvis and whispers in his ear. Elvis says, "He wants me to tell you that he says thank you to everyone for helping him when his life was in danger and he hopes to be back on duty welcoming guests to Bunnyland as soon as possible." More applause.

Rex manages a weak wave and, as rehearsed, attempts to rise from his wheelchair but quickly slumps back down again, looking exhausted. Dr. Nick fusses over him and tells Elvis that they must cut short the press conference because they don't want to risk a relapse.

This carefully staged cameo performance has the desired effect; the TV and press reporters are happy with the coverage they've got, while Bunny Warren Junior wipes away his tears, as do all the other executives, keen to be seen to follow suit.

Later, Rex Rabbit tells Elvis that he owes him a huge favour for getting him out of a lot of trouble. What can he do for him in return?

The Colonel suggests that they should make a single together, featuring an amusing take on an old Elvis song, 'Bunny Honey'.

Elvis pulls a face as if he has just eaten something very unpleasant and retorts, "Oh no, that is just so corny."

The Colonel, always able to think quickly on his feet, says, "I told Bubba that it was a rubbish idea but he insisted on me putting it forward." Shaking his head sorrowfully, he says, "That boy's got a lot to learn."

"One-two-three-kick, one-two-three-kick," shouts the director. "C'mon Elvis and Rex, pick it up. And you Bunny Girls in the chorus line, let's get those kicks really high and wiggle those tails. C'mon, pep, more pep."

Rex Rabbit's idea as to how he can repay his debt to Elvis is for them to do a charity show to raise funds for the children's zoo at Memphis, and rehearsals are now under way. The Bunnyland Corporation is very happy to be associated with such a project since it ticks all the right boxes – children, animals, a good cause, famous guest stars, and wholesome family entertainment.

Unbeknown to them, however, Colonel Parker has engineered a fly in the ointment with a spot for his Dixie Chickens act which will see them dancing on a straw-covered hotplate to 'Sweet Georgia Brown'. There is more good news as far as the Colonel is concerned when Elvis agrees to perform 'Hound Dog' to Charlie Hodge who will be dressed up in an Old Shep costume which the Colonel has had made and which he wants him to wear once the Elvis theme park opens. The outfit is woolly and heavy and, as part of his feud with Charlie, the Colonel will make sure that it is draped over a red hot radiator for hours right up until the moment he steps into it.

"What with him being under the stage lights, I reckon he'll dissolve right away into a small puddle," he chuckles to himself.

"Miss Merman, you're up next," calls the director, and 'There's No Business Like Show Business' blares out over the loudspeakers.

There is one incident that threatens to spoil the rehearsals when the munchkins learn, while running through their performance with Ann-Margret who is guesting as Judy Garland in the 'Over the Rainbow' number, that the Colonel has put them on half-pay. They're dwarfs, so half size, half pay, he maintains, and he torments them further by keeping on singing, 'Grumble while you work, Grumble while you work, You're on half-pay, That's what I say, Grumble while you work' until they can't stand it anymore and, like an angry swarm of hornets, they race across the stage and start punching his knees. The situation is finally resolved thanks to the intervention of Elvis and Rex Rabbit and the Colonel's reluctant acceptance to pay up.

The climax of the show that evening, which will ultimately raise tens of thousands of dollars, sees a baby elephant, loaned by the Memphis Zoo as its contribution to the event, emerge from stage left.

No one knows what causes the elephant to lift its trunk high in the air and make a couple of loud trumpeting noises; maybe it's the lights or the noise of the audience that make it nervous. But it suddenly bolts across the stage, causing the munchkins to dive into the orchestra pit to escape being trampled, while the Bunny Girls scream and run backstage. The elephant is nonplussed for a moment, having gone as far as he can go, so he decides to charge back the way he came, causing Old Shep (as played by Charlie Hodge) to join the munchkins by leaping into the orchestra pit.

Like bullfighters Elvis and Rex Rabbit duck and dive out of the way of each charge to shouts of "Ole" from the audience. Then Colonel Parker suddenly trundles across the stage clutching a dancing chicken under each arm and yelling, "Save my girls!"

The audience thinks that the madcap chaos they are witnessing is a beautifully choreographed finale to the show and they are all on their feet laughing, clapping, stamping their feet, whistling, and shouting "Encore! Encore!"

Elvis has an idea, runs backstage, and returns with a box of donuts that he retrieves from his dressing room. He tosses a donut towards the elephant who immediately stops to eat it and looks around for the next one. Elvis empties the box onto the stage and while the elephant keeps popping donuts into its mouth, his keepers are able to get him back under control.

Elvis nods towards Rex Rabbit, Ann-Margret, and Ethel Merman, and together they walk to the front of the stage ready to apologise to the audience. But as Elvis is about to try and say sorry for the shambles they have just seen, a young guy steps forward and tells them, "Please wait there. I want to say something on behalf of everyone here. We all agree that this show is the funniest thing we have ever seen. Congratulations to you and all the other performers. It was magic."

The guy turns round to face the audience who all cheer and shout "More! More!"

"We're all agreed," he tells Elvis and the other performers. "We will happily pay the ticket price all over again just to watch that finale one more time because it was priceless."

"What do you think?" asks Elvis, turning to the other three. "It might be a very hard act to follow."

Ends

8. Garden Party Monkey Business

"More grits anyone?" asks Minnie Mae, pouring a thick stream of honey into the pan and adding a large knob of butter. Instantly, the calorie count shoots up higher than the Dow Jones Index.

"They surely do look good an' ready," she adds, giving the grits another stir.

Elvis passes his plate to his grandmother for another helping as well as asking for some more waffles.

Priscilla sighs; she finished her breakfast of a diced carrot and three slices of cucumber some time ago. She is becoming impatient, tapping her long red fingernails on the table in the kitchen at Graceland, wanting to reveal her Big Idea that is going to elevate Graceland from the showbiz section in the magazines to the high society pages.

"Elvis, honey, could you just leave the waffles for a minute," she requests. "And Charlie, please stop washing up. I've got something important to say."

Charlie Hodge looks distressed as he wipes his hands on his floral pinafore. "I don't want to get behind. I've still got the Jungle Room to do. Elvis and the boys were in there last night watching a big ball game."

"I get it, Charlie. It will look like Skid Row. But leave it for now."

She tells them that she has read in a magazine that she and Elvis are America's royal family and that Graceland is their palace. Presidents and their first ladies come and go, here today and gone tomorrow sort of folks, and in any election, nearly half the people don't vote for whichever president wins anyway. But unlike them, says the magazine, Elvis and Priscilla, as the King of Rock and Roll and his Queen, are universally popular. Their status is secure in ruling the hearts of the American people.

"That's a real nice way of putting it, I think," she comments.

The magazine then goes on to talk about the life of the British Queen and the garden parties she organises in the grounds of Buckingham Palace and the sort of people who come as her guests. She walks around, carrying her handbag on her arm, chatting to them; afterwards she gives them some sort of picnic. It is a high point of the social calendar and an honour to be invited as a guest. Can the Presleys fulfil a similar role in the lives of Americans, ponders the magazine.

"So," she says. "I think it would be real nice and classy if Elvis and I were to have a garden party here at Graceland. If it works for the Queen, then it surely can for us. And when we go to the Royal Highland Games in Scotland next year, as assuredly we will, the Queen and I can chat about our garden parties, you know, and swap ideas and recipes."

"I think it is a mighty fine idea," declares Elvis. "But what's Colonel Parker going to think? He's not mentioned it to me before."

"Frankly, I don't care diddly squat what he thinks. My mind's made up. We're doing it." She looks around the kitchen at each one in turn with a steely not-to-be-contradicted stare.

Minnie Mae, who is Elvis's grandmother, thinks they are going to have to provide a lot of food for a lot of folks, so she'll scrub out one of the bins and make a big stew. She can also wring the necks of a few of the turkeys that they keep in the grounds of Graceland.

"That sounds like one of those Tupelo clambakes from the good old days," says Vernon, Elvis's father, who was on the verge of nodding off to sleep but is now quite animated. "Maybe we can get Aunt Delta to set up a still."

Priscilla smiles and slowly shakes her head. "We going to save ourselves a lot of trouble," she tells them. "For the kind of folks who will be coming, we need to offer them something dainty and classy, not chitlins in a basket and hooch. We're going top of the range. Me and Minnie Mae will sit down and study the Piggly Wiggly supermarket's banquet catalogue and all we need to do is tick a lot of boxes and they'll deliver it all to Graceland."

Colonel Parker is distractedly pulling at the lever of the gaming machine in his office, using it as if it were a string of worry beads. The news of the garden party has not gone down well. What is the point of it? A lot of people will be turning up to freeload and fine dine at Elvis's expense; in his mind, he imagines a Jacob's ladder of invoices piling up and up towards the sky. It is why he needs the consolatory feel of his gaming machine in his hand to help calm him down and come up with an angle.

The door opens and he uses his crumpled straw trilby to waft away the thick clouds of cigar smoke to reveal his assistant Bubba.

"How on earth am I going to take care of business with this garden party stunt of Priscilla's?" he grumbles. "It's all expense, expense, expense. It's ruinous." As if to underline his state of mind, he brushes away an imaginary tear.

It is a routine Bubba has seen often before. Nevertheless, he tries to appear sympathetic and concedes that it is a puzzle. But Priscilla insists she wants it to be a classy affair, so she has banned the auctioning of invitations, raffles, any form of gambling, and stalls that sell cheap Elvis memorabilia.

"Cheap!" roars the Colonel, almost yanking off the handle of the gaming machine in his disgust. "They're the heirlooms of the future."

"Careful, sir, remember your repetitive strain injury."

The Colonel shakes his head wearily and says he can take a pretty good guess as to some of those who will be on the guest list: The Mayor, the Chamber of Commerce, the Temperance Society, the Daughters of the Revolution, Mr. and Mrs. Dull…

"I believe you would have more fun picking up litter in a cemetery than going to Priscilla's garden party. Where's the excitement, and the thrill that you get when you can play a few games of chance to boost the party mood?"

Bubba repeats that Priscilla wants it to be a high society affair, polite and discreet, and she has also lined up a very special guest.

"Let me guess – it's Mother Teresa," sneers the Colonel. "Well let me tell you, Bubba, I'm now thinking of inviting a VIP guest myself. Somebody very, very special. It certainly will be a surprise.

I can't wait to see Priscilla's face. You'd better make sure that Dr. Nick is standing by with the smelling salts."

He resumes his seat behind his desk, feeling much cheered by his plan. He pats his vast stomach that is reminiscent in its size to Ayers Rock; if he were living in Australia he would be a tourist attraction in his own right; photographs would be taken of him and appear on postcards.

He takes a phone call to confirm that the Dixie Chickens, his dancing chickens act, will be performing at the annual Carny Convention in a Palm Beach casino, confident that their new sand dance routine is better than anything Wilson Keppel and Betty can do. As an insurance policy he has gone to the expense of buying a new hotplate on which, when covered in straw, they will dance.

Colonel Parker is listening to the radio and as soon as he hears Elvis singing 'I Forgot To Remember To Forget' he knows that this is the cue he has been waiting for. As the song finishes, the DJ, George Klein, announces that his old school friend and best buddy Elvis and his wife Priscilla will be having what they are calling a garden party at Graceland.

"And get this folks, they will be welcoming a very special visitor. We are talking here about someone who is Very Very VIP. Someone who will be there By Appointment! Got it yet?" teases George.

He starts to play another Elvis record while Bubba, utterly perplexed, asks the Colonel what on earth is he talking about. What VIP visitor? Has this come from Elvis or Priscilla? Do they know what is going on?

The Colonel smiles enigmatically, leaning back in his chair with his hands resting on his stomach that is so big that the fingers of his hands cannot touch. He is the epitome of smugness, feeling so pleased with himself for coming up with a scheme that will score a little victory over Priscilla in return for her insistence on organising the garden party when he was opposed to it. She will learn who is the one who takes care of business. If he wasn't so fat he would hug himself.

George Klein's voice moves up through the octaves as he shouts, "Oh Lawdy Miss Clawdy! The VIP guest at the Graceland garden party is none other than... now remember folks, you heard it here first from George... yes I can reveal that it will be the Queen of England herself. I know everybody has just gone into shock. So I'm going to repeat that. Queen Elizabeth of England. Yes, she'll be heading for Memphis. You'll know her because she is famous for her curly red hair and very white make-up. And you heard all about it first from George on Radio WHBQ." He puts on another Elvis record.

Bubba cannot believe what he is hearing. He manages to stutter, "He's t-t-talking about the Queen c-c-coming to G-G-Graceland. That's impossible."

"You just heard it from George Klein himself," responds Colonel Parker, dismissively waving his cigar in the air.

"No, C-C-Colonel, you don't understand. What I mean is she c-c-can't c-c-come because that's the wrong Queen Elizabeth. The red-headed one's been d-d-dead for more than 400 years."

Colonel Parker suddenly hurls his cigar to the floor, clearly wishing that it was George Klein's face he was grinding into dust with the heel of his shoe. "That idiot hasn't got the brains of a gnat. You've always got to do everything yourself. I'll get on to the William Morris Agency myself and make damn sure they send the right double for the right Queen."

"But Colonel, don't you think you should rethink this?" pleads Bubba. "Remember that Priscilla wants everything to be classy and done in the best possible taste. This doesn't sound like such a good move to me."

"What's more classy than having the Queen of England attend your garden party?" he retorts. He lights another cigar, takes a few puffs, and sighs deeply. "I guess you're right, Bubba, the more I think about it. Remind me to call the agency to cancel the Queen booking. Meantime, if Priscilla comes looking for me, say I'm away at an important business meeting."

It is the perfect day for a garden party. Graceland looks elegant and regal; it is possible you can believe you are standing in the gardens of Buckingham Palace itself. Charlie Hodge has been busy arranging the tables and chairs in clusters around the grounds; he has ironed the white linen tablecloths and napkins, and given an extra polish to the cutlery and glasses that gleam and sparkle in the sunshine; a line of tables is set up and covered along its entire length with all the finest ingredients of a banquet that the Piggly Wiggly supermarket can provide. The guests in their smart suits and dresses stand and chat; Minnie Mae has had her hair permed and, for the first time in years, she has forsaken her dungarees to wear a dress; Vernon has bought himself a new white Stetson hat, and Aunt Delta has promised to stay sober.

Although Colonel Parker is yet to be seen, evidence is found of his attempts to introduce some 'fun' to the event. When the security people carry out a final sweep, they discover some roulette and craps tables hidden beneath blankets and a saddle in the stables. And alongside the table where the invitations are checked as the guests arrive, a stall selling 'genuine' Elvis rings and silk scarves is also taken away.

Priscilla smiles and thinks to herself that Colonel Parker must be mad if he thinks he can get away with his cheapskate money-making tricks on such a special day at Graceland. Not on her watch!

Elvis tells a press conference that he and Priscilla are pleased that the story about the visit of the Queen of England has been cleared up. "It was just my old buddy George Klein having a bit of fun," he says. "I mean, it had to be a joke, didn't it? George tells me he knows that it is impossible for the real Queen to come anyway, although of course, she'd be made reeeal welcome, but she needed to be at the state opening of Harrods in London."

Priscilla has opted for a dark red suit with a pearl necklace and earrings. Her bouffant hair has been back-combed and lacquered into a chrome-like sheen; it is piled as high as a guardsman's busby and if a force 10 gale were to suddenly spring up, not a hair would be blown out of place. She feels happy in the warmth of the sun and the glow of satisfaction that everything is going well and to plan. Earlier, she and Elvis welcomed the

Governor of Tennessee and the Mayor of Memphis. Now, Elvis is chatting to a group including Sam Phillips, of Sun Records, and the Blackwood Brothers who will be providing some suitably uplifting entertainment later in the afternoon.

She says "Hi" to the movie producer Hal Wallis and his wife who tells her what a swell party it is. "We're still looking for Colonel Parker," says Hal. "He is here, isn't he?"

"Why of course! How could we possibly have organised such a garden party as this without the Colonel." She smiles sweetly but there is an edge of acid in her voice.

She thinks she sees the disc jockey George Klein in the crowd and wants to tell him all is forgiven concerning that silly announcement about the Queen coming to the garden party. She will assure him that she suspects who is really to blame, but when she looks again, he has gone.

There is loud cheering from the sightseers at the gates as they open and a white limousine, as long as a bowling alley, makes its way slowly up the incline to the house.

Taking Elvis by the arm, Priscilla leads him to the portico of Graceland so they can greet her special guest. As the limousine draws to a halt, out from the back steps Liberace in a white suit encrusted with jewels and sequins, with black and white piano keys on the lapels, and a long pure white ermine fur coat that trails yards behind him. Elvis, who is wearing his white sunburst jumpsuit, looks dowdy in comparison. From the front of the limousine steps brother George with a silver candelabrum which he holds aloft and displays to all the guests as if it were the newly won Superbowl trophy; he is followed from the opposite side by their mother, Frances.

When Priscilla politely admires her gown, she replies that Walter, which is how she calls Liberace, told her that Mr. Dior had personally flown it out to her for the occasion. "I just love French fashion, don't you," she says. "So chic."

"It's gorgeous," says Priscilla, fixing a smile, but thinking it looks like the sort of thing – all frothy and floaty – that Ginger

Rogers wore in the 1930s when dancing with Fred Astaire. Maybe it is a Dior museum piece. She informs Liberace's mother that Edith Head had flown in from Hollywood especially to design her outfit.

While Elvis and Liberace chat about their forthcoming shows in Las Vegas, promising to go and see each other perform, brother George pulls out a monogrammed 'L' handkerchief, gives a polish to the candelabrum, and asks which table they will be sitting at.

Nobody loves animals more than Elvis. At Graceland, there is his ancient hound Old Shep, horses in the stables, and a dozen or so turkeys that scratch around under the trees on the knoll. So it comes as no particular surprise when he returns home one day with another pet, although admittedly the fact that it is a chimpanzee does cause a bit of a frisson.

Elvis bought him from a guy standing on a corner near The Peabody Hotel. "The little fellow looked so sad and needed cheering up so I gave the man 100 dollars and brought him home," says Elvis. The chimpanzee gets his name of Scatter because everybody immediately scatters as soon as he comes through the door because he leaves a trail of destruction in his wake whenever he appears. One of the first things Elvis did was to take him to the Lansky Brothers store to get Bernard to run up some chimpanzee-sized jumpsuits. At one time, a place used to be laid at the table for Scatter who was served with the same meal as everybody else, apart from Priscilla, that is. But he was more likely to jump on the table and hurl his food at the walls than eat it. Elvis would hoot with laughter and this seemed to encourage Scatter who would screech, scamper across the table and seize something from a plate. He would often finish the meal swinging from the curtains.

On one occasion, there was a road accident in Beale Street involving three cars and a pick-up truck that the drivers claimed was caused by the shock of seeing a chimpanzee, dressed in a white jumpsuit and cape, driving a Cadillac; the chimp, they said, was accompanied by a guy wearing an old fashioned yachting cap, but the police dismissed the whole thing as being preposterous and it was hushed up.

However, the family decided that lines had been crossed and enough was enough. It was explained to Elvis that Scatter was suffering from constipation, a condition he well understood and with which he could sympathise; he agreed that Dr. Nick, his personal physician, should take charge. Dr. Nick made sure that Scatter became much calmer and never suffered from constipation. A paddock was found in some remote corner of the grounds and Scatter was forgotten about – until now...

No one knows how he got out – did somebody release him or did he simply escape? Certainly, there are a lot of theories afterwards about what might have happened. But there he is standing next to Elvis, holding on to a trouser leg.

After being welcomed by Elvis and Priscilla, Liberace notices Scatter. "Hey there little fella," he says and bends down to pat him on the head. Scatter thinks he'll do the same and reaches up to put his hand on Liberace's head only to find that he is holding his toupe.

Liberace yells and attempts to cover his head with his hands, while Scatter, suddenly frightened, screeches and races away still clutching the toupe. He leaps onto the banquet table and runs along it, screaming and baring his teeth, while still holding Liberace's toupe. One foot lands in the egg salad, and a few yards further on, he steps in the trifle, before dropping the toupe into the punch bowl where it slowly sinks to the bottom beneath various floating pieces of strawberry, orange, and cucumber.

Vernon, who has been drinking the punch, lifts the toupe out with a pencil, wrings out as much of the punch as he can into the bowl, and with it perched on the end of the pencil but still dripping slightly, he walks towards Liberace's limousine.

While Scatter ran off in one direction, Liberace raced towards his limousine, locking himself inside and closing the curtains. When Vernon taps on the window, the car door opens a couple of inches, and a hand reaches out and takes what looks like a bedraggled dishcloth rather than a $1,000 toupe.

Once Liberace has removed bits of fruit and wrung every possible drop of punch from it, he beckons Vernon to come closer and says, "Tell George to bring the candelabrum. Let him know

I'll be ready in a moment or two. And do you think I can borrow your Stetson hat?"

A minute or so later, there is more tapping on the car window and Liberace asks irritably what is the matter because he is not quite ready. The tapping continues so he pulls back the curtain. "Yes?" he inquires.

Suddenly a face looms close to his on the other side of the glass and Liberace lets out a terrified shriek. Continuing to tap on the window, like a vampire seeking to be let in, is a woman with vivid red curly hair, a face that looks as if it has been daubed with white emulsion paint, blood-red lips, and a lace ruff as big as a tyre around her neck.

"Hi," says the creature to Liberace, who is cowering in his seat and backing away as far as he can, wondering what other disaster can befall him. "I'm Queen Elizabeth. Is this the Presley's garden party because I'm expected?" Which circle of hell is responsible for organising garden parties, Liberace asks himself? What more can I endure?

Later, Liberace has regained his composure and is now wearing his toupe again, thanks to brother George being able to smuggle it into Graceland hidden in Priscilla's handbag; there he was able to give it a wash and blow dry with her hairdryer.

He puts a hand on Elvis's shoulder and says he wants to let him into a secret. "I'm not really bald at all, you know."

Elvis nods sympathetically and confides that he knows as much.

Liberace explains that he needed to have a minor surgical procedure on the top of his head. This required his hair to be removed, and his surgeon recommended that a toupe be worn as protection to aid the healing process until his own hair grew again.

"Thank you, Lee, for explaining it," says Elvis, who is trying really hard to keep a straight face. But then he collapses in a fit of giggles. "But it was a hair-raising experience, wasn't it?"

He apologises for what was a silly, tasteless spur-of-the-moment joke. "I'm so glad that we've had this conversation. Because otherwise, I would have gone through life, totally incorrectly, thinking that you were bald."

"You see, Elvis, appearances can be deceptive," comments Liberace, with a wan smile. "We're lucky, you and I, to have such handsome heads of hair. I mean, take that wonderful, lustrous black hair of yours…"

Liberace wonders what happened to the so-called queen who frightened the living daylights out of him.

Elvis bursts out laughing again, saying she had to leave the party in a hurry. "I'm sorry you missed it, Lee. It looks like Scatter has learned a new trick because he snatched her curly red wig off her head and ran away with it up a tree. Everybody was laughing because ole Scatter was up there trying to fit it on his head. The poor queen's face was redder than her wig."

He adds, "The final touch came from your brother George. He spread a coat on the ground for her to walk over on her way out."

Ends

9. "You Tarzan and Me Jane"

Hal Wallis has flown in from Hollywood especially to say thank you to Elvis and Colonel Tom Parker. "You have probably saved Paramount Pictures and me as well," says the man who has produced many of Elvis's movies. "I am eternally grateful."

Work on his latest blockbuster movie 'Animal Magic: The Story of St Francis of Assisi' has been suspended midway through production after two of the stars were caught in a debauched motel room scandal, a situation made much worse because the picture is being partly financed by The Vatican.

"I had the Pope himself on the phone," mourns Hal Wallis, holding his head in his hands. "I don't speak Italian but I could tell he was as mad as hell, and pardon me for saying that."

But with no word from The Vatican and no work being done on the movie, he is left with a menagerie of animals being kept on a backlot at Paramount, munching their way through what is left of the budget. "I'm telling you, boys, they live better than the guests at the Beverly Hills Wilshire. Then there's the wages of the curators, the vets' bills…" His voice trails off as he wrings his hands in despair.

However, he has come to Graceland to discuss a plan that he and the Colonel have dreamed up for a Tarzan movie. Their logic is that they've got a Tarzan – Elvis, of course – they've got the animals, they can get stock jungle footage to go with the sets, and Hal's team of writers will have a script ready by the end of the week. The Colonel says that he or his assistant, Bubba, will talk to the William Morris booking agency to find a Jane that Elvis can work with, hopefully, Ann-Margret or Tuesday Weld, someone who will look good in a jungle style swimsuit.

Once Elvis has left the meeting to go to lunch, the Colonel says he wishes to mention a delicate subject; he is concerned about

Elvis appearing in a skimpy loincloth such as worn by Johnny Weissmuller. But Hal Wallis reassures him that the Tarzan in this movie will appear in a tiger skin jumpsuit with flares and a cape.

It is the first day of rehearsals of the new Tarzan movie and the door slides open to the sound stage on the Paramount Studios lot in Hollywood and in sashays Mae West, followed by her three maids struggling to drag large suitcases containing her make-up, gowns, and hats. Elvis is wearing his Tarzan jumpsuit, while Mae West is in a shimmering silver gown that fits like a skin and displays a cleavage as deep as the Grand Canyon. Her hips sway from side to side like a pendulum, hypnotizing Elvis who stands open-mouthed, immobile like a statue, apart from his eyes which move from side to side in synchronisation with her hips.

She slowly looks him up and down. "Mmm, hello big boy," she says with a smile that's almost a smirk, "You Tarzan and me Jane", words that make Elvis feel that Dracula has just rested a hand on his shoulder and invited him to dinner.

She purses her lips together in a kiss and flutters her eyelashes which are so long that Elvis feels the draught.

Colonel Parker and Hal Wallis look at each other utterly perplexed, holding out their hands in a gesture that asks: what is she doing here?

(The explanation is that when Bubba, the Colonel's assistant, rang the William Morris agency in New York about casting a Jane for Tarzan he is asked where they will be doing the filming, to which he replies, "Not entirely sure at this stage, but we may go west." He means, of course, Hollywood, but Mae West is jotted down on the notepad and the agency, being so super efficient, draws up her contract in next to no time and that's how she gets the part.)

"Hi, Hal, long time no see."

"What a lovely surprise to see you, Miss West," he replies nervously.

"Mmm, I do like a man who's enthusiastic. I'm here to put some sizzle into your new movie."

Hal puts on his straight face, the one he uses when he plays cards with the Colonel. "Is that right? You say you're in this movie? I must admit the news comes as a big surprise to me and I'm the producer, so if you don't mind, just as a precaution, I'll have the contract checked out."

"Hold on Tiger, it's tighter than your wallet. Listen, my little chickadee, save your energy for something more exciting such as when I'm feeling less tired."

She points out that she usually writes the script for the scenes in which she appears, adding, "You know, Hal, you can rest easy. I've still got it at 49."

"49! 49? What 49 years?"

"Mmm, that's right. I was just a kid in those early movies of mine."

One of her maids brings her an 18-inch long cigarette holder which Mae directs towards Hal and waggles it at him. Finally, he gets the idea and lights the cigarette. She blows a little smoke into his face and says, "Mmm, thanks Hal. I like a man who takes his time but eventually gets it right."

Then she sashays over to the Colonel and asks him if he used to serve in the Air Force.

"No Ma'am, I'm a Colonel in the regiment of the Virginia Fencibles."

"I thought it must be the Air Force because you're built like one of those barrage balloons that float around in the air. But don't worry, honey, because I know how to get a man in shape."

She oozes back towards Elvis who is still standing silent and stock-still with his mouth so far open he could catch a whole swarm of flies. She links her arm in his and leads him towards the centre of the sound stage.

"You don't say much, do you honey. But talk is cheap and I've got expensive tastes. Don't worry, I like strong silent types."

"Thank you Ma'am," Elvis manages to blurt out, paralysed with fear.

Mae West begins to outline to him her ideas for the movie, and they include a lot of snappy one-liners, innuendoes, a hootchy-kootchy dance and a jungle wedding.

"Why don't you come and see me some time in my trailer and we can… er…rehearse a few things," she says with a wink. "They say practice makes perfect."

Elvis tries to free his arm from her grip but it is as if he is being held by a clamp. "That sounds great, Miss West, but don't you think we should run it by Colonel Parker and Hal Wallis first."

Mae West is never going to miss the opportunity of telling the world of her first starring role in many years and the one that can relaunch her career in the movies; she intends to shout it from the rooftops. Within 24 hours of arriving on set, she is on the phone to Hedda Hopper, who reveals in her Hollywood column that as well as starring as Jane she is also working on the script of Elvis's new Tarzan picture. And just like in her heyday, there are the classic Mae West quotes in the article like, "Some folks call me a Rolex because I like a good time and I can party around the clock, and oh boy, that Elvis makes every second count."

Colonel Parker is enjoying a few hands of gin rummy with Hal Wallis in a quiet corner of the set when he is told that Priscilla is on the phone and wants to speak to him urgently.

"What's this old has-been doing in a picture with Elvis?" she shouts. "She was making pictures before 'Birth of a Nation'. And have you read what's she's saying about her and Elvis in the newspapers? What's going on there? Is anybody in charge?"

The screeching is so loud he has to hold the phone away from his ear, but he is able to make out that she is furious about what is going on and if he does not sort it out immediately, she will turn up there herself and fix it.

"I promise I'll get this done right away or I'm a Dutchman."

Then, realising what he has just said, he coughs and says, "Oops," but Hal Wallis pretends he didn't hear anything, although he is aware of the rumours about the Colonel's background.

Elvis has taken to spending more and more time in his trailer with the curtains drawn, brooding on how he has ended up with Mae West as his co-star and not Ann-Margret, Tuesday Weld, or Shelley Fabares. His mood darkens when he hears an insistent knocking on the door and the words, "Elvis, sugar pie, it's your little chickadee come a-calling."

The knocking becomes louder. "Elvis, it's our playtime," she shouts. "and I've got some new games for us to try."

Charlie, his old friend and faithful gofer, believes he has an idea worthy of Jeeves himself and, wiping his hands on his floral pinafore, he opens the various locks on the door and tells her, "He's not here. He's out. He has taken Cheeta, (Tarzan's chimpanzee) for a very long walk."

"Mmm, I don't think so, my little elf," replies Mae West. "Cheeta is right here with me and he's looking at me with his big sad eyes and saying where is Elvis?"

Charlie is crestfallen that his ruse has been shot down in flames and he can hear Elvis cursing to himself inside the trailer.

Mae West is not going to be put off, because she sees Elvis as the means to resurrect her career and, if she can glue herself to him, provide her with a golden future – her second coming.

She calls to her maids to set up a table and chair outside Elvis's trailer. "Ladies, please bring me a cocktail while you serve lunch right here." She spots a corner of a curtain being lifted, waves and winks in an exaggerated way, and then turns towards her maids and shouts, "And bring something for the monkey."

The three maids work in shifts around the clock, sitting at the table and watching the trailer to make sure Elvis doesn't leave without Mae West being there to intercept him.

"It's just like I'm in prison," complains Elvis, morosely eating his last donut. "I've been turned into the Count of Monte Christmas, gaoled forever."

Charlie peeps outside and sees one of the maids smiling broadly and waving at him. "Miss West is on her way in a new outfit to show Elvis," she shouts.

He makes a gesture with his feather duster and turns to Elvis, "You know that Count guy you mentioned, I believe he did eventually escape."

He is cheered up by this information, but then Charlie adds that he thinks it took him 17 years before he dug his way out of his prison.

Elvis cringes when he hears a knocking on the trailer door, but it is followed by the announcement, "Lunch for Mr. Presley" in a voice he does not recognise.

One of Hal Wallis's make-up girls is making the delivery and the boxes she brings contain a cowboy outfit and cosmetics, although Elvis is disappointed that his usual burgers, fries, and chocolate milkshake lunch seems to have been forgotten.

She asks Elvis to put on the cowboy outfit and, once she has done some work on his make-up, she gets him to practice his walk up and down the trailer until he gets it right. "Remember, Elvis, his walk is very distinctive."

Hal Wallis and Colonel Parker have been busy plotting not only how to get him out of his trailer but also how to break Mae West's contract. The pressure is really on because Ann-Margret has created a gap in her schedule. There is now a window in which she can play Jane, so they need to resume shooting as soon as possible.

The make-up girl confides to Elvis that the ground is being prepared for Mae West's downfall, tapping her nose in a knowing sort of way. It is all being very carefully choreographed and Hal Wallis will fill him in on the details.

When Mae West turns up in a full-length, tight-fitting gold dress and a large hat topped with ostrich feathers, she asks her maid if she has seen anything of Elvis.

"No ma'am. The only person I've seen, apart from the girl delivering lunch, is John Wayne. He came out of the trailer a while ago, tipped his hat to me, and said, 'Howdy' and 'Where's my horse?' When I said I didn't know he said 'he must have gone thataway' and walked off towards the sound stage."

"Hmm," says Mae West, putting her hands on her hips and tapping her foot. "I smell a rat. You say he went thataway."

When she arrives on the set she asks Elvis if John Wayne is appearing with them in the movie. "That'll be the day," Elvis retorts, and at a signal from Hal Wallis, a trap door suddenly opens beneath her and she disappears with a crash, followed by a scream.

"Mae West has left the building," one of the crew, rather cruelly, calls out.

The trap door exit was well prepared and she lands on piles of cushions so that she is not injured, but she does emerge looking dusty and bedraggled. The studio doctor and medical team, who are also in on the act, are summoned to treat her. The doctor shakes his head and makes a lot of tut-tutting noises, while Mae West insists she is not badly hurt. However, his opinion is that she may be suffering from a delayed concussion and she needs to be admitted to a clinic at once, followed by four weeks' complete rest.

"What about me being in the movie?" she demands to know.

There is a sharp intake of breath from the doctor and more shakes of his head. They cannot take any risks with her health.

"Can I get a second opinion?"

"Yea, you can have mine," replies Hal Wallis. "We can't ignore medical advice. I'm sorry Miss West."

"OK, Hal, then I'm gonna sue you and Paramount. I'm gonna be like a giant vacuum cleaner, sucking up piles of damages."

She turns to the doctor to remind him to be careful where he puts his stethoscope and that any bandages he applies must be pink – her signature colour.

Elvis begins to cough, and having gained everyone's attention, he wonders if he might have a private word with Miss West.

He points out to her that she is a singer as well as an actress, and if it will help her career while she recuperates and awaits her next film role in what, he assures her, will be Hal Wallis's very next production, he will use his influence to secure a deal with a top label for her to record a solo album. And as part of the deal, he will sing a duet with her to be released as a single.

"Mmm, you're very persuasive," she simpers. "I hope you are not taking advantage of me."

Priscilla marches into the Colonel's office at Graceland where he is in a meeting with Elvis and slaps a newspaper on his desk and tells him, "I'm being sorely tested. We've been here before and I really did think you'd killed off these kind of wild stories."

She jabs a long red fingernail at the headline which reads, 'Mae West loves Elvis's Great Balls of Fire'.

She glares at them both. "What the hell does she mean? Care to tell me what's going on?"

"Ah," says Colonel Parker who, on seeing the expression on her face, would dearly like to try to hide himself under his desk, like people were once taught to do in the event of a nuclear bomb explosion. But, of course, he is too big to squeeze under there.

"Oh," adds Elvis. "Satnin' (his pet name for his wife) it's a song, honey, that's all. She told me she wanted to do something raunchy so that's what we sang…"

But she cuts him short. "Listen, Elvis, and you too Colonel. This is it. Mae West is done. Finished. Finito. Over. Got it!"

She storms out of the office, slamming the door behind her with the force of a minor earth tremor.

Elvis fiddles with the fringes on his jumpsuit, and mumbles, "I think she really means it."

Colonel Parker picks up the phone and calls his assistant. "Bubba, we've got a major problem and we need to postpone – no, better play safe and cancel the 'Elvis Goes West' tour… And the spot they're booked to do on the Carol Burnett Show? No, I don't know if the Tiny Terror watches it but I'm not taking a chance, so yea, cancel that too… I know it is all a bit last minute, but something has come up… And what if Mae West calls… well, I'll try and think of something."

Ends

10. Colonel Parker goes into Rehab

"No No No. You cannot do this! Who are we dealing with, the Gestapo?" thunders Dr. Nick. "On behalf of my patient I must protest at this outrage."

The nurse explains to him and to Colonel Parker that inspecting the contents of a suitcase is perfectly routine. The Pat Boone Friendly Persuasion clean living clinic and rest home is dedicated not only to helping people to rest and recuperate but also to overcome their addictions.

She points out that in the past patients have tried to smuggle in all sorts of things from boxes of pizzas to whisky disguised as bottles of mouthwash and, on one occasion, a hookah pipe. Such contraband must be confiscated for the patients' own good.

As if on cue, on lifting up a large pineapple patterned Hawaiian shirt, she suddenly lets out a gasp, puts her hands to her mouth, and staggers backwards. She could have been posing for Edvard Munch and his painting 'The Scream'. At first, she struggles to find the right words as she points at the roulette wheel in the bottom of the Colonel's suitcase. Finally, she manages "What is that?"

"Ah, that'll be down to my young assistant Bubba," Colonel Parker explains, shaking his head sadly. "You see those numbers around the edge of the wheel. That fool boy must have thought it was my calculator. An easy, honest-to-goodness mistake to make, I'm sure."

Once the roulette wheel has been removed, the Colonel and Dr. Nick, Elvis's personal physician, who has accompanied him to the clinic, are taken on a guided tour, including the common room where all the patients sit in plastic-covered armchairs in a circle around the edge of the room, facing inwards towards each other, many of them with a zimmer frame close to hand. Apart from a few snores and the Pat Boone songs being played softly on a tape loop over the PA system, it is as quiet as a Trappists' committee meeting.

"Oh Lord, what do people do for fun around here – take an embalming class," Colonel Parker mutters to himself. "This place is going to need livening up before we all petrify."

Finally, they are taken to his own 'I'll Be Home' suite. The nurse says the clinic was surprised to receive a medical certificate signed by Dr. Nick that Colonel Parker, for health reasons, must be allowed to smoke cigars. However, the only place that he will be allowed to smoke is here in his suite where they've turned off the sprinklers. Before leaving, she wonders if there are any of the 'A Wonderful Time Up There' recreation classes he'd like to sign up for. He thinks he'll wait and see.

Urged on by Elvis, Colonel Parker has finally agreed to be booked into the clinic to try and find a cure for his addiction to gambling and a condition described by Dr. Nick as gambler's palsy. It may be a repetitive strain injury that causes his hand to shake as a result of playing for too long on gaming machines. But the Colonel's assertion that his hand doesn't shake when it is clutching the lever so he must be OK is dismissed as irrelevant by everyone at Graceland. One of the problems with the Colonel's gambling habit is that he is a perpetual loser. Perhaps it could be disguised or even overlooked if he were to win sometimes, but he never does. He is the most popular gambler in the United States, welcomed everywhere, the one person everyone wants to play – because he never wins. Yet he passionately believes that he is only ever one pull of the lever or one turn of the cards away from a transformative big win.

Elvis is genuinely concerned about him and wants to help, hence paying for his stay at the Friendly Persuasion clinic. Pat Boone is known to be a clean-living, god-fearing guy and so this should be the ideal place for his rehab. He has long suspected that his Las Vegas concerts may be linked to the Colonel's gambling debts, thus allowing him to be there to gamble for hours and weeks on end while Elvis is performing. But he also knows how much he owes to Colonel Parker who has made him the

King of Rock and Roll, a top rank Hollywood movie star, and the most successful entertainer in the world. There probably isn't a street anywhere in the world that he can walk along and where he won't be recognised and welcomed. So whatever his problems, that is all down to the Colonel.

Now that the nurse has left, Dr. Nick, smiling like the Cheshire Cat, places his briefcase on a table. He lifts the lid with the flourish of a magician producing a rabbit from a hat. It is full of packets of different coloured pills. He taps the side of his nose with his finger and says, "By all means follow the clinic's instructions for rest and recuperation, but these pills are the magic that will cure your shakes. These are my little miracle workers. I'm Elvis's doctor, trust me."

He explains his Rainbow therapy: red pills for getting to sleep; orange pills for waking up; yellow pills to soothe his nerves; green ones to help his appetite; blue for blood pressure; indigo for indigestion; and violet to combat hair loss. And this is the clincher: each pill contains a laxative so there is no risk, because of a change of diet, of the Colonel becoming constipated, something, he believes, that is so important for his overall health and recovery. The Colonel offers his thanks, but of course, he has no intention of taking any of them.

In the Jungle Room, Elvis is having his final fitting for his costume for his part in Hal Wallis's next movie to be titled 'Mary Queen of Scots'. Bernard Lansky, a tape measure around his neck and a cluster of pins in the lapel of his jacket, is putting the finishing touches to a jumpsuit in a Royal Stuart tartan complete with a short cape, raised collar – and another nod to Scottishness – a white lace ruff at the neck. Bernard insists that because Lord Bothwell (the part to be played by Elvis) is married to a queen, his clothes need to reflect his status and to make him stand out, so he has overlain the jumpsuit with lots of large silver sequin thistles. Finally, he puts on Elvis's head a tartan tam o'shanter with a peacock feather tucked into the headband to complete the ensemble.

Charlie Hodge, Elvis's old friend from Army days, is also there, having appointed himself as Elvis's voice coach. As part of the process, he and Elvis have been watching Scottish films and TV shows like 'Whisky Galore' and 'The White Heather Club'. His theory to sounding like a native is to say och aye a lot and put Mc in front of some of the words. That should Mcdo it, for instance, he laughs.

Hal's writers started work on the script a couple of days ago and some of the early scenes have already been sent to Graceland for Elvis to read through.

While Elvis and Bernard Lansky, who has been designing his outfits since his days at Sun, check out his appearance in a full-length mirror, Charlie finds a page and reads aloud: 'Queen Mary enters the hall of a Scottish castle and Lord Bothwell (that's you, Elvis) bows low'. He studies the dialogue, while stroking his chin, and says Elvis should say something along these lines: "Och aye, greetings to mah McQueen from her loyal Mchusband."

Elvis nods approvingly. "What do you think boys, does ole Charlie here sound like a Scotsman?" he calls out to Red and Sonny West. However, the cousins are both sound asleep in a far corner of the Jungle Room. In the cause of Scottishness, they have turned to drinking whisky instead of beer, ever mindful of knowing the value of taking on board whatever trend Elvis is following. The problem is that they have been supping it as if it were beer. So instead of being occasionally unconscious, they are now catatonic most of the time.

Priscilla pops in to remind Elvis that he has promised to visit Colonel Parker at the Pat Boone clinic. Elvis, thrilled with his new costume, strikes a dashing Bonnie Highland Laddie pose.

"Och aye, what do you Mcthink, Priscilla?"

"Why Elvis," she tells him, "if I close my eyes I could swear I was listening to Robbie Burns himself. And if I open them wide, then I do believe I am looking at a scene straight out of 'Brigadoon'."

After she has left, Charlie tells him that it seems he has passed the Scottish accent test and he is now good enough to be taken for a Scotsman in Glasgow on a Saturday night.

"Yea," agrees Elvis. "I'll fly us there once filming is over and we can have some fun mingling with the crowds. It might help me to blend in with the locals if I go about wearing this costume. And maybe while we're there we can visit the glens around Prestwick and meet up with my relatives from the Presley clan."

Colonel Parker is bored out of his mind sitting in the common room at the Friendly Persuasion clinic watching a rerun of a Pat Boone Show on TV. Then, as if a starter gun has been fired, many of the patients sitting in chairs around the room start to clamber to their feet, with some of them grabbing for their zimmer frames. They all begin to shuffle and clunk their way towards the toilets. It is like watching a flock of panic-stricken sheep bunching around the gate of a pen and struggling to force themselves through as quickly as possible. The nurse who has been sitting in the corner quietly doing her knitting is now urgently ringing a bell and summoning assistance to find out what is going on. She should ask the Colonel who is smiling for the first time since he has been at the clinic. With no intention of taking Dr. Nick's pills, particularly in view of their constipation-busting side effects, he has been handing them out to the other patients who thought they were chewing brightly coloured sweets. The dash – if that's the word – to the toilets shows how wrong they were about what they were taking. For the Colonel, not only is it an amusing break in the tedium, but it gives him an idea.

His first venture is to organise zimmer frame races in the common room with bets placed on who – eventually – wins. There is quite a bit of excitement among the competitors and the spectators, who much prefer the Colonel's idea of fun to watching Pat Boone on TV. However, the races can take a while to complete, and one or two of the competitors have fallen asleep before the finish. Over the next day or two, to make things more interesting, he introduces a system of handicaps, with the so-called 'faster' competitors starting a little further back than the rest, with the result that the finishes are much closer, the excitement increases, and so does the number of bets.

While the residents are parked in their chairs by the nurses to watch TV and have a sleep, the Colonel runs a book on some of the programmes; for instance, how long it takes into an episode before Colombo lights up his first cigar.

At lunchtime, the nurses hear numbers being shouted out all around the dining room. '25' is answered by '31', then '19' and '28' all of which are duly written down by Colonel Parker in his notebook. The staff can't figure out what is going on. Is it some kind of bingo? But how can that be? They are simply eating their lunch and not crossing out numbers on cards. So what is going on? In fact, the patients are betting on how many peas there are on their plates, with cash prizes being paid out afterwards in the common room to the highest and lowest scores.

What concerns the doctors and nurses is that the usual zombie-like existence of the residents has changed overnight. Their state of easily manageable semi-permanent stupor has been replaced by a general mood of hyperactivity and hilarity as they wait to bet on the Colonel's next game. And the games are coming thick and fast. No one is resting in what is supposed to be a rest home, none of the addicts are being cured, and even those who are supposed to go home at the end of their stay are refusing to leave because they are having so much fun.

Of course, it is too good to last.

Elvis is relaxing on a green faux fur sofa in the Jungle Room, still dressed in his Lord Bothwell costume, contentedly working his way through a tartan tin of shortbread biscuits, believing that this will help him become more Scottish. Bubba pops his head around the door and says Elvis is wanted on the phone by the Friendly Persuasion clinic where the Colonel is staying.

The doctor introduces himself and explains to Elvis that Colonel Parker needs to leave immediately and will he come and collect him.

"But he hasn't been there very long. Surely he cannot be cured already."

"To tell the truth, Mr. Presley, he's probably incurable. He is a disruptive influence who is, we believe, having a harmful influence on the well-being of the patients and the running of the clinic and rest home. We have had to inform Mr. Boone of our concerns. He is deeply shocked."

"This is incredible. He went there to get better and find a cure for his gambling addiction. What on earth is going on?"

"Wait a moment Mr. Presley while I hold the phone to the door of the common room and you may get some idea."

"What is all that hootin' an' a-hollerin', doctor. It sounds like a Wild West saloon on a Saturday night when the drinks are on the house."

"Exactly Mr. Presley. This is supposed to be the time when they do their jigsaw puzzles. But we believe that Colonel Parker is at this moment organising a zimmer frame line dancing competition and that he is taking bets on the outcome. You're in films. You may be too young to remember that scene in 'Destry Rides Again' when Marlene Dietrich gets in a fight in the saloon. Well, what is going on here is a bit like that in terms of rowdiness. So we'd appreciate it if you could be here as soon as possible."

Elvis leaves immediately, so he is still wearing his Scottish costume when he arrives at the clinic.

"Is it Burns Night, Mr. Presley?" the doctor inquires, rather sniffily.

Elvis explains it is for his new film and he was at Graceland trying it out to see how it feels and looks when the doctor's call came, so he decided to leave at once rather than get changed.

The Colonel is sitting in the lobby, his suitcase by his side, and when he sees Elvis and Charlie (who has accompanied Elvis so he can carry the Colonel's suitcase) he greets them with a wave of his straw trilby.

The doctor asks Elvis to step into his office so that he can talk to him privately. He points out that the purpose of the clinic is to help its patients to overcome their addictions and to rest and recuperate. But quite the reverse seems to be happening since Colonel Parker has set himself up as some sort of entertainment officer and bookie.

"But is there any evidence that proves that Colonel Parker is actually behind all this?" asks Elvis.

"That is sort of difficult to answer. We spoke to one patient who said she wasn't leaving here until she had finished her 'learn to play poker' lessons that she has paid for. Naturally, we questioned her about who she has paid, but – let me just check my notes... yes, here it is... her answer was 'I'm pleading the Fifth Amendment'. Can you imagine some elderly patient saying something like that? And that's what we are up against – a wall of silence."

Elvis points towards a glass jar on the doctor's desk that has three snails inside which has aroused his curiosity.

"Again, it is the same story, Mr. Presley," replies the doctor. "What can you definitely prove? A nurse found these snails on a shelf in the common room. If you look carefully, each one has a number painted on its shell. Were they used for racing? Was betting involved? You tell me, Mr. Presley. But I do believe that there has been a profound change in the atmosphere here and the behaviour of our patients since his arrival and that things will be a lot quieter after Colonel Parker has left."

Elvis nods his head and adds softly to himself, "And maybe a lot duller."

The doctor takes a letter from the drawer of his desk; it is from Pat Boone and he asks him to give it to Colonel.

Back in the lobby, Charlie picks up the suitcase while Elvis hands over the letter to the Colonel. He knows better than anyone else how these things work and this letter has not been within 100 miles of Pat Boone. It will read as if it has been written by a committee of lawyers and will indemnify the Friendly Persuasion clinic against everything, including World War Three and the liability of returning any fees. It is not worth the paper it is written on so he screws it up and uses it to light his cigar.

"Hey you can't do that here!" shouts a nurse running towards him.

Too late. The smoke drifts up and sets off the fire alarms that begin to ring throughout the building. Nurses rush from room to room shouting 'don't panic'. Then the sprinklers come on.

Despite the racket, you can hear the sound of zimmer frames being clumped across the floor and above the hubbub, some of the patients are calling out that if this is another one of the Colonel's games they want to get a bet on.

Ends

11. Hamlet: Not To Be

Hal Wallis has been having the toughest couple of days he has ever had as a movie producer. He's known as the fastest man in Hollywood, the Jesse Owens of the movies, the producer who holds the record for finishing a full-length feature in the quickest time.

He always comes in under budget and the finance guys in New York love him; putting money into one of his pictures always returns a profit. It's his photograph they have framed on their desks, alongside those of their wives. Hal is ultra-careful with money and the ship he runs is so tight it could be in corsets. But for once, this particular ship is heading for the rocks because work on his latest movie production, a rock opera of Shakespeare's 'Hamlet', is in danger of turning into a tragedy.

Knowing how well similar Shakespearean projects such as 'West Side Story' and 'Kiss Me Kate' have done in the past, the movie producer has high hopes of a similar box office triumph: Elvis and Nancy Sinatra in the lead roles, the kudos of producing what is regarded as Shakespeare's greatest play, and an album's worth of songs. How can it fail? But from the first day, things start to go awry.

He complains to his wife Martha in a phone call to their home, "I feel like I'm the captain of the Titanic. People are running for the lifeboats, the orchestra is playing something mournful and I'm heading for disaster in the shape of two icebergs, one called Elvis and the other called Nancy Sinatra."

"Listen, Hal, sweetie, don't be so gloomy. You've only just started work on it. What's it been – a couple of days? How can it be so bad? Remember that Elvis movie 'Easy Come Easy Go'? It was a Thanksgiving Day size turkey. But you made good money on that picture. You turned lead into gold so I reckon that makes you a genius. Okay, so this picture might not be another 'Casablanca' for you, but you'll turn it around."

"I'm worried that this will be a financial flop – the first of my career. The money men in New York will say I'm losing my touch. I don't want this to be some awful swansong. I don't want my epitaph to be about a rock opera that hits the rocks and sinks without trace."

"Hal, don't beat yourself up. You'll get it right – you always do. Call me again tomorrow. But I've got to go now. I'm holding a Tupperware party and I'm on a commission on everything that's sold."

When Elvis first heard that Hal Wallis intended to produce Shakespeare's 'Hamlet', he didn't know much about either the writer or the play, but hey, from what little he did know, he believes that this can be his breakthrough role, the chance to demonstrate his talent and to be taken seriously as an actor. He is convinced he can be another James Dean. They are alike in so many ways that they could have been brothers. Like Dean, he is a rebel, he has the same brooding good looks and an innate acting ability. All he needs is to be given the right role.

He is really keen to make the critics eat their words, those who said about his movies, 'What does $1 million of ham look like?' and 'They need to get the drains fixed at the movie theatre because there was a dreadful stink during the showing of Elvis's latest picture'. Cruel jibes engraved on his heart.

He tells Charlie Hodge, his oldest friend and loyal gofer, "It is something I have always wanted to do – to act in a heavyweight role." Charlie thinks to himself, but would not dare mention it, that Elvis has the heavyweight side of things already taken care of.

Elvis is disgruntled. "I feel unfulfilled and I need the chance to shine and show the critics that I really can act. I know it's just a dream, but what if the famous Sir Laurence Olivier was sitting there one day, watching me and telling me afterwards, 'Elvis, they've got it all wrong. I can see for myself you're a damn fine actor'. Wouldn't that be swell."

But when Hal Wallis reveals that 'Hamlet' is going to be a rock opera, it quickly transpires that his manager Colonel Parker has committed him to doing yet another movie musical stuffed with hack songs, albeit with a trickier script than usual. With his acting hopes seemingly once again crushed, it is hard to work up much enthusiasm for a film that will probably emerge from the sausage machine just like 'It Happened At The World's Fair' or any of the 30 others.

Hal Wallis seeks to reassure him that he has got it all wrong, that it is an entirely new concept, one that will be seen as a cultural landmark, the 'Citizen Kane' of movie musicals.

Colonel Parker takes a different approach, reminding him that nobody pays any attention to what the New York critics say; they're a bunch of Ivy League snobs who are out of touch with real folks.

"We're in the business of making happy pictures – ones that make the people who watch them happy. And as for the people who produce the pictures and those who show them in the movie theatres, well, they are happy too because your films always make money. Go ask Hal, or Jack Warner, or Louis Meyer, if he were still alive, God rest his soul, and they'll tell you that the first law of Hollywood is to make money. Anything else is a bonus."

Things start to go wrong on the first day when the Hamlet costumes are unveiled. Hal claps his hands for a male model to make his entrance wearing what will be Elvis's outfit. He sashays to the centre of the studio floor, pauses with his hand on his hip, turns left and then right, tosses his head, and sashays back out again.

It was always going to be hard for Elvis to whip up much enthusiasm for the part anyway, but he is horrified at what he is supposed to wear. He explodes, "Tights! You want me to wear tights! I'll look ridiculous! No sir."

The producer attempts to patiently explain to him that this is how Hamlet traditionally appears – in black doublet and tights. He will be following in the footsteps of all the great actors who have played the role. Sir Laurence Olivier and Sir John Gielgud, for instance, always dressed this way. Surely he must realise that this is what is required if he is to write another memorable page in the history of theatre.

But Hal's rhetoric washes right over Elvis who shakes his head and mutters, "tights... Elvis don't wear tights." The next day he turns up in an outfit designed and made for him overnight by Bernard Lansky; it is a black velvet jumpsuit with flared trousers, high stiff collar, black cape with red satin lining, and on the chest, a large representation of what is supposed to be Yorick's skull. "Now I look the part," asserts Elvis, at ease in his usual style of outfit.

"El, you look the smartest, classiest Hamlet there's ever been," pipes up Charlie.

Hal Wallis is convinced that Elvis's opposition encourages Nancy Sinatra to dig in her heels when she sees her Ophelia costume, which is a dark red, full-length dress with long sleeves, specially made for her by top costume designer Edith Head as a favour to Hal.

"It's the sort of thing some old gal who's a resident of a Miami retirement home might wear," she sneers. "You know, by the way, Hal, that I never appear without my long white plastic boots – they're my trademark. I can't upset my fans. Unless I get to wear these boots then I'm made for walking – right off this set."

Like Achilles in his tent at Troy, fulminating on the injustices inflicted on him by Agamemnon, Hal's two stars retire to their trailers to brood on the iniquities of their costumes and their roles.

With just 25 days budgeted to complete the filming and editing, this kind of surly resistance from his stars is not what Hal Wallis needs. To succeed, the movie has to flow like one of Henry Ford's conveyor belts.

The crisis causes the old problem of his dyspepsia to flare up; he feels as if Mount Vesuvius is about to erupt inside his stomach. His face goes red, beads of sweat pop out on his brow, and he has to chew on a couple of tablets which he takes from a tube in his pocket.

He gets on the phone to his lawyers, instructing them to do whatever it takes to find a 'doublet and hose' clause in Elvis's contract and a 'no boots' one in Nancy Sinatra's.

However, Colonel Parker, a good friend because they have worked together on so many of Elvis's other movies, urges caution; perhaps he should try and find a compromise. There is no way that he will be able to persuade Elvis to wear tights, but he might be able to get him to agree to the rest. Similarly, he should consider letting Nancy Sinatra wear her white boots which probably won't be visible under her long dress.

The Colonel recalls the time that she and Elvis were making a movie called 'Speedway' with another producer. There was a problem with the electricians union; the men downed tools and no work was taking place. Nancy happened to mention it to her father, saying that the movie, which was important to her career, was in jeopardy of not being made. Almost immediately the strike was over after its leader electrocuted himself and was in hospital for a week. Fancy that, people said afterwards, an electrician like him having a faulty toaster in his home. Although he was generally fine afterwards, he never lost the permanent look of shock on his face – eyes wide open and his eyebrows soaring upwards like the Golden Arch in St Louis. The moral of the story, says the Colonel, is they don't want Nancy calling her daddy to fix things. They should do what they do best – find a solution to the problem, cut a deal, and then get on with the picture.

The next day, when Elvis appears on the set, the movie producer sees that Colonel Parker is as good as his word and a compromise has been reached with Elvis's costume. But he must admit it is a strange-looking ensemble, a fashion mongrel of the 1600s and the 1970s. Elvis is wearing a tight-fitting black doublet with a row of small, silver buttons running down the front from the neck to the waist with what look like aerofoils sitting on top of the shoulders. The tights have been replaced by the black velvet flared trousers that were part of the outfit made for him by Bernard Lansky.

Just as Hal Wallis finishes his first sigh of relief that they can get on with the picture, Elvis, clearly troubled by something, taps his finger at a page of the script. He confesses that he is struggling to make sense of the 'to be or not to be' speech.

These theatre actors must really earn their dough, he says. The speech is like one of those Peter Piper tongue-twisters in which he himself can never get beyond 'pickled' before screwing up. And if that's not bad enough, he can't figure out what on earth Hamlet is trying to say anyway or why he's even saying it in the first place.

"I mean does anyone have a clue what this is all about?" He gazes around the set but everyone else is looking away and making a point of being busy doing something.

He frowns and strokes his chin. "I think it holds up the action, so my suggestion is that I look to the camera and say 'to be or not to be... I'd better think about it a bit more and make my mind up later'. And that's it – no more and no less. To me it feels like the guy is in a bit of a bind and doesn't really know what to do. So if we cut the dialogue right back like this, I believe we capture in a couple of sentences the essence of what's a very long and hard-to-understand speech. Otherwise, the whole scene sags. I reckon moviegoers will thank me."

Hal Wallis wrings his hands and puts on his best ingratiating smile. He has won a small victory with the costume, so perhaps a degree of patience is called for.

"You see, Elvis, this is the most famous speech in the whole play. Everybody knows it and they'll all be waiting for it, wanting to see how you do it. I know we're filming a rock opera and not a stage play, but we just can't do 'Hamlet' without 'to be or not to be'. The critics will kill us."

Elvis shudders at the mention of the word critics and his face blanches.

Hal explains that it would be like Elvis ending his show and not singing 'Can't Help Falling In Love' or Judy Garland not performing 'Somewhere Over The Rainbow'. It can never happen because it is such an integral part of the experience for the fans. Similarly, this speech is such a fundamental part of the play that people will feel something has gone terribly wrong if they don't hear it in full.

Hal walks over, puts a fatherly hand on his shoulder, and says, "Elvis, you're a great star and a great actor. I know you can do this."

"Excuse me, can I make a suggestion?" interrupts Charlie, holding his hand up hesitatingly, as if he were in class.

There is a stunned silence on the set; everyone is shocked at the possibility that he may have an idea. It is unheard of; it is unprecedented.

Colonel Parker is the first to react. "I don't think anywhere needs cleaning for the time being, Charlie. You can put your duster away."

But he persists, "I just thought that perhaps we can ask Sir Laurence Olivier when he gets here how he thinks Elvis should do the speech."

There is an audible gasp, eyes goggle, and jaws drop faster than elevators heading for the basement. Of course, Charlie may have got the whole thing wrong, but what if he is right and the greatest Shakespearean actor of the 20th century is heading their way? Fear and panic begin to spread like a miasma across the set.

"Just thought I'd ask, Charlie, but when are you expecting him to be here?" wonders Hal, nervously.

He looks at his watch. "In about half an hour."

With his dyspepsia suddenly raging like a wildfire on a California hillside – hot, windy, and out of control – the producer takes a couple of tablets from the tube that he now wears on a chain around his neck as if it were a pair of glasses. He is now chewing so many that there is a permanent fringe of white powder on his lips and the cast and crew are getting worried about what might be in the tablets and are on the lookout for any signs of irrational behaviour.

"But Charlie, answer me this: why is he coming here?" demands Elvis.

"You said it was always your dream to have Sir Laurence Olivier sitting there to see you act this part. I thought you must have forgotten all about it. But because it is so important to you, I used my initiative and invited him to come to the rehearsals."

"Charlie Hodge used his initiative. Oh no, we're all doomed," mocks the Colonel.

Everyone looks daggers at Elvis. Luckily for him, they are not real, otherwise he would be skewered to the floor. Hal looks this way and that, as if searching for a place to hide, while the Colonel mops his brow with a faded King Creole handkerchief and tries to disappear behind a screen of cigar smoke.

"Look everybody, it was a joke," explains Elvis, turning this way and that and spreading his arms wide in a gesture of submission. "When I said that about Sir Laurence Olivier I was being ironic."

"Should I phone my daddy," asks Nancy Sinatra.

"No, please don't do that, Nancy," says Hal Wallis. "It's all hands on deck. We need to put on some sort of show. Remember, he can sink us with a couple of comments in the press. Come on, we can do this."

Sir Laurence Olivier arrives promptly on the set in a morning suit, winged collar shirt, cravat, gloves, and spats, all in different shades of grey. He looks as if he has come directly from an audience at Buckingham Palace. Having introduced himself, he sits on a chair in the centre of the set, taps his silver-topped ebony cane on the floor several times, and announces, "begin."

They start with a reading of the ghost scene that will open the movie. Next, Nancy Sinatra steps forward as Ophelia in her long dress and white plastic boots, sighs deeply and admits that she is feeling blue and low down. She proceeds to sing a song that is very much like her big hit 'Sugar Town' and finishes by saying she is going to look for a stream to fall into. There are a lot of whoops and hollers from everyone on the set, clearly moved by her performance, but Sir Laurence looks as if he has swallowed a wasp.

As Elvis walks onto the set, the famous actor flings a hand across his face, as if to protect his eyes from a powerful spotlight that has been suddenly trained upon him. Then, slowly, he parts two of his fingers to take a peek.

Sensing that this pantomime has something to do with his costume of doublet and flared trousers, since he has not yet uttered a word, Elvis asks him, "Well, do you like wearing tights?"

Sir Laurence couldn't be more shocked than if someone had pushed a custard pie in his face. "Wear tights? How dare you! I don't know what you mean. I am a perfectly normal Englishman."

"No, I mean when you play Hamlet."

"Ah, now I understand. Yes of course I do. Everybody does who plays Hamlet. It's like a uniform that goes with the role. Now we have cleared that up, please begin."

Elvis decides to take Hal's advice and to read the full version of the 'to be or not to be' soliloquy rather than his own much-abridged version. He goes for the full James Dean treatment with added angst and eye-rolling and as he finishes, he adds that at this point the script requires him to sing a song along the lines of his mother being a mean, black-hearted no good woman.

There are more cheers from everyone on the set, diplomatically just a little bit louder than those for Nancy Sinatra since Elvis is the main star of the movie. Everyone now looks to Sir Laurence for his verdict.

He starts by saying he was promised an exciting new interpretation of 'Hamlet', something never seen before in the theatre, at least according to someone called Charlie who invited him to come. Has anyone seen him, by the way? Everyone immediately looks for Charlie who quietly slips out of sight.

"Having just seen what is admittedly only a short rehearsal, I must tell you quite candidly that you have failed in your objective," he pronounces, removing a handkerchief from the sleeve of his jacket and loudly blowing his nose as if the whole experience has been particularly distressing.

"When the world's greatest scholars sat down to decide what is man's finest artistic achievement, it was not Michelangelo's Sistine Chapel that they chose. Nor was it Beethoven's 5th Symphony. Do you know what they selected? Shakespeare's 'Hamlet'. That play is regarded as the pinnacle of man's artistic achievements. But what have you succeeded in doing to it?"

He turns his head and holds his hand up to his ear. "Do you hear that whirring noise like a washing machine that's getting faster and louder? That is Shakespeare spinning in his grave."

"So I'm guessing you didn't really like it," says Elvis.

"As a project, I think your version of 'Hamlet' is definitely not to be."

There is a huge disconsolate sigh from everyone on the set, like a large balloon slowly deflating and somebody, presumably a stagehand, blows a loud raspberry. Hal Wallis takes another couple of tablets from the tube around his neck and pops them into his mouth to quell the riot fomenting in his stomach.

Elvis walks over to him and tells him, "I'm sorry we let you down with this one. But here's to the next picture. I'm always happy to work with you, Hal. Maybe we just have to get used to sticking to the same old formula. Perhaps this one was just a bridge too far."

The producer is genuinely touched by Elvis's kind words and turns to everyone on the set. "I apologise everybody. I had great hopes for 'Hamlet' the rock opera, but perhaps we should listen to someone as distinguished as Sir Laurence when he tells us it's a bummer."

"Pardon me, ladies and gentlemen, but would you mind just waiting a moment," says the celebrated actor. "Perhaps your efforts have not been entirely wasted. You have given me the germ of an idea that may just work."

He explains that they should focus on the plot of 'Hamlet' and what it offers as a movie – a murder, an investigation to find the killer, more bodies, a ghost on the loose, a spooky old mansion, digging around in a graveyard...

"Hal, maybe you and I are the only ones who might remember that old film 'The Cat and The Canary' with Bob Hope and Paulette Goddard. Do you know what I think? That we can come up with an even better comedy murder mystery film than that, one loosely based on 'Hamlet' that will better suit Mr. Presley and Miss Sinatra. And we can do it in modern dress and ditch the tights."

Then he adds, with a bit of a smile, "And perhaps there can be an English detective who works with them to help find the murderer."

Hal Wallis splutters in disbelief, "You don't mean..."

"Actually I do," responds Sir Laurence. "I'm over here for a few weeks and would be available – if required."

"If required!" Hal snorts with laughter and shows his delight at this turn of events by dancing a jig, causing some of those there to wonder again what is in the tablets he keeps taking.

"The detective's name could be Toby O'Notterby," calls out Charlie who is encouraged by the good news to emerge from his hiding place. "D'ya geddit? To-by O-Not-ter-by," he chuckles.

"Who is this rather small person," says Sir Laurence, examining him intently as if he were a laboratory specimen, "attempting to make a rather feeble joke?"

Elvis tells him that it is his very good friend Charlie Hodge, the person who invited him to come to the rehearsal.

"Oh dear," declares Sir Laurence, recoiling and removing his handkerchief from the sleeve of his jacket and patting his nose. "Perhaps we can find him a small part in our film, perhaps as a gravedigger."

Everyone laughs uproariously as if it is the funniest joke they have ever heard.

The actor knight volunteers to direct the movie since it is something he might find amusing; Hal Wallis, Elvis, and Nancy Sinatra readily accept the offer, and the producer says his writers will have a shooting script ready in 72 hours.

Sir Laurence doesn't want any songs, apart from possibly a duet over the opening credits which, of course, is a disaster as far as Colonel Parker is concerned, since it wrecks the usual album tie-in deal with an Elvis movie. For the time being, Sir Laurence can do no wrong, but the Colonel is not finished yet. Oh no. He flicks away the cigar ash which has accumulated like tumbling scree down the front of his Hawaiian pineapple pattern shirt and sets his mind to coming up with some sort of rescue package to make up for the disappearing dollars. Maybe he can shoehorn in an extra song to make two sides of a single that can be released. Or run a 'Knight for a Day' competition in a newspaper, with the winner spending a day on the set with Sir Laurence Olivier and Elvis – with something that says 'if they are available' in one of the small print clauses near the bottom.

Or better still, he'll ask Sir Laurence if he likes to play cards. He'll be busy because he's both directing and acting in the movie, but there is always some downtime while scenery gets shifted and sets are rebuilt. He'll invite him to join him and Hal Wallis for a few friendly hands of poker, and he'll teach him to play the game which he'll call the Shakespeare shuffle Texas hold 'em. Kindergarten stuff, he'll assure him, and the Shakespeare connection should spark enough interest to get him hooked.

At least his old friend, Hal Wallis, is a happy man. The Mask of Tragedy has turned its face to the wall, to be replaced by the beaming smile of the Mask of Comedy. A movie is being resurrected from the ashes.

Hal phones home to tell his wife, "Wait till I tell the money men in New York about my new movie starring Sir Laurence Olivier and Elvis. They'll be throwing dollars at me. You can give up the Tupperware parties."

"Damn!" declares Colonel Parker, hurling his cigar to the ground and stamping on it. And with that much weight bearing down on it, what is left of the cigar stub is reduced to a residue of ash as fine as face powder. "How did it happen? We got suckered in and he played us like a violin," he curses to Hal Wallis. Their poker game with Sir Laurence Olivier does not go anything like as planned.

How they chuckle and rub their hands excitedly when he agrees to play. "He's supposed to be a great actor, so let's see how he acts when we take him to the cleaners," grins the Colonel, puffing on his cigar like a locomotive building up a head of steam. But in fact, they find themselves caught like fish flapping helplessly on the end of a line.

Before a hand has been dealt, they know that something is going seriously wrong. Sir Laurence performs a trick that neither of them has ever seen before or thought possible. While he is shuffling the cards, one of them, as if pulled by some invisible string, suddenly leaps in the air from the pack and comes down face down on the table. He asks the Colonel to turn it over: it's the ace of spades. While he continues to shuffle another card spirals into the air and falls onto the table. He nods to Hal Wallis, who turns it over: it's the ace of hearts. He performs the trick two more times, and out fly the ace of diamonds and then the ace of clubs. Colonel Parker and Hal Wallis look at each other and gulp. The Colonel pushes his yellow straw trilby to the back of his head and mops his brow, and Hal takes one of his dyspepsia tablets, at the same time wishing he could think of an urgent appointment elsewhere.

Hal settles his debt by agreeing to an increase in Sir Laurence's fee for the picture. Then, after the Colonel has written out his IOU, the actor knight – who declines a cheque to be drawn on the Jefferson Davis Bank – discloses that he learned to play poker when he was offered the part of Lancey 'The Man' Howard in the movie 'The Cincinnati Kid'.

He explains that he couldn't do the film in the end because of a commitment with the National Theatre in London. But, as he says with a smile, all the trouble he took learning to play poker for the part was not wasted. It is like riding a bike – something you never forget.

"Oh my, that was fun," he adds. "Shall we play again tomorrow?"

Ends

12. GI Blues

It has been 24 hours since Elvis opened the letter informing him that he is being drafted into the armed forces. He is devasted, convinced that his career is over. It is so unfair because he has hardly got started, he complains. He is also desperately worried about the impact that it will have on his parents, particularly his mother.

"Two years – that's how long I've gotta serve. Two years. It's like a life sentence," he says mournfully. "By the time I leave the forces, folks will be saying Elvis who? They'll have forgotten all about me. I'll be washed up at the age of 25."

At this his mother Gladys bursts into tears again; she has hardly stopped sobbing since Elvis first read out the letter. "Do something, Colonel Parker. I'm begging you. You're his manager, you're supposed to take care of things," she pleads.

His father, Vernon, tells him, "You've gotta go right to the top. Go to the Pentagon and get this fixed. You're a Colonel. They're bound to listen to you."

Colonel Parker is deep in thought as he tries to figure out a rescue plan. As part of his contemplative routine, he strokes several of his chins, or as many as he can fit into the palm of his hand at one time, and pushes his yellow straw trilby to the back of his head with the end of his cigar, fortunately not the end that is alight.

He points out that Elvis was passed 1-A in his medical examination at the Memphis Draft Board, and that's a big barrier to get over because it rules out going back and claiming he should be exempt on medical grounds such as flat feet or an allergy to gunmetal.

"I think Vernon's got the right idea. I'm going to go to the Pentagon and talk to the top brass and see what can be done.

There must be an angle I can find. But whatever happens, I want you all to know that I'll be there marching alongside Elvis every step of the way."

Minnie Mae, Elvis's grandmother, emerges from the kitchen carrying a stack of pancakes topped with double cream and maple syrup. She is trying to keep up his spirits by making his favourite meals. She's also been busy baking a triple chocolate and fudge cake with chocolate icing for when he has finished the pancakes.

"Ah do declare, ah'm a-thinkin' to mahself Elvis should serve his time with that thar Sergeant Bilko," she announces. "Y'all can see on the TV that he surely do like a-bein' in the army an' he has a whole heap o' fun. That'll suit Elvis jest fine, ah reckon, a-bein' with Sergeant Bilko."

"Yes! Yes! Yes!" shouts out Elvis's mother, who has suddenly stopped crying. She claps her hands with delight and says, "That's the answer, son. You go right ahead and serve in that nice Sergeant Bilko's platoon. We can watch you on TV once a week and it'll put my mind at rest. Then I can see for myself that you're doing just fine and I won't miss you quite so much. Yes, son, you do it. That way I won't be fretting about you."

Elvis recognises what a difference this utterly impossible idea has made to his mother. It has stopped her tears and made her a lot happier about what is going to happen to him. He simply does not have the heart to tell her the truth, at least not for now, so he nods meaningfully at Colonel Parker and decides to play along.

"I used to drive a truck so I'm betting that when they send me to Fort Baxter they'll want to put me in Sergeant Bilko's motorpool," he jokes ruefully.

His mother beams happily and gives him a hug. "When you get there say hello for me to that Private Doberman, won't you. He's such a funny guy."

The scheme to get Elvis drafted into the armed forces began to take shape a couple of weeks earlier in the White House.

Seeing that President Eisenhower has nodded off in his chair behind the desk in the Oval Office, Vice President Richard Nixon tells the President's two aides, "I think we are going to have to wake him up if we're going to get this plan through now."

"Okay, you know the drill," says Nixon. On his signal, the three of them start to cough, quietly at first and then increasingly louder until the President wakes up.

Eisenhower begins to stir, yawning and rubbing his eyes as if he is emerging from hibernation.

"Sorry to disturb you, Mr. President, while you are deep in thought on important government business," says Nixon, "but there is something we need to run by you and get your authorisation. We have to do something about Elvis Presley, sir."

"Who?"

"He's a popular entertainer, sir," one of the aides informs him.

"You mean like Bing Crosby."

"Not quite, sir."

Nixon explains that Elvis has outraged all decent people in America with his rock and roll music and his obscene gyrations while performing on stage. Articles and pictures about him fill every newspaper and magazine. You cannot switch on the TV or the radio without seeing and hearing Elvis, and now he is making films in Hollywood. He is like a universal rash – everywhere and very unpleasant. Parents, teachers, and church leaders complain he is corrupting the youth of America and he has to be stopped to save them from a headlong plunge into hell.

Bringing his indignation nicely to the boil, Nixon reveals that the DOORMATS and the SODS are threatening to stage a protest march on the White House. The President looks perplexed as he tries to picture doormats marching through Washington DC, possibly with a 'Welcome' on them.

"Daughters Of Our Revolution Making America Triumphant Society, DOORMATS, sir, Sons Of Decency Society, SODS," explains Nixon as patiently as possible. "These are big organisations, Mr. President, and every single member is a dyed–in–the–wool Republican."

Turning on the fawning unctuousness that would make Uriah Heep blush, he continues, "We need their support. Unhappily for America, sir, you will have to leave office after two terms. The Grand Old Party needs to find a successor who, without your immense popularity and dynamism, is going to need every single vote."

The two aides, Chuck and Steve, shake their heads sorrowfully and add, "It's sad but true, sir. Without you, every vote counts."

"So what are we going to do about this Elvis Presley then?"

"You're going to draft him into the armed forces. He'll serve for two years and by the time he gets out everybody will have forgotten all about him. Just sign here… and here."

"The army – that's a good career. He'll love it. Look how it worked out for me," muses the President, pleased that they are making such a good choice for him.

The two aides beckon to the Vice President and whisper to him, "Isn't the draft supposed to be a lottery? How do we know Elvis Presley will get picked?"

"C'mon guys, get real," snaps Nixon. "The draft is whatever we want it to be. Mr. Presley will be drafted."

Nixon informs the President that they should ultimately send him to serve in Germany where he will be a long way from the USA and the nation's teenagers.

"This is a very smart move, sir," declares the Vice President. "Congratulations. You are taking decisive action to lance the Elvis boil and it will appeal to millions of right-thinking Americans. And, mark my words, it is going to be worth a landslide of votes. You have just insured the future of the Republican Party and the United States."

"Yes sir, in one move you are rebalancing the moral code of Young America," echo his aides.

The President looks pleased with what he has accomplished. "It's been a busy morning, hasn't it? Is there anything else I should be doing or signing?"

They assure him with this business taken care of he is now free for his daily round of golf and his playing partner today is Bob Hope.

He chuckles, "Luckily for me he's not like that Elvis Presley you've been warning me about, is he?"

"No sir, you'll be fine. He's one of us," his aides tell him.

The four generals representing the army, navy, marines, and the air force come straight to the point: Which fool had the brainwave of drafting Elvis Presley into the army as a GI?

"Well…" says Vice President Nixon, pausing to hear what more they have to say before committing himself. The Pentagon has requested the meeting in the Oval Office as a matter of the utmost urgency, but what can be the problem? After all, it is a vote winner. Lots of Americans will happily wave goodbye to Elvis.

Because, continue the generals, who have enough stars on their uniforms to form a small constellation, this utterly stupid decision will cost the armed forces hundreds of millions of dollars.

Nixon swallows hard and fights to suppress the panic suddenly building up inside him. Has he put a foot wrong somewhere that might just jeopardise his political ambitions? As always happens in times of stress, he starts to sweat. "Hundreds of millions of dollars, you say? How?" He unbuttons the top of his shirt and runs a finger round the inside of the collar.

It is hard to put an exact figure on the amount, the generals tell him, but it is a starting point. So how did this happen, they demand to know?

Nixon thinks the time has come for him to live up to his nickname of Tricky Dicky. He glances at the President's two aides, Chuck and Steve, nods his head, and simultaneously all three turn to look at President Eisenhower who is concentrating on the doodles he is drawing on his writing pad. It is difficult to tell but it appears as if he is trying to design a golf bag.

"Please tell us what the problem is so that, er, the President can put things right."

Elvis Presley, the generals continue, should have gone into the Special Services. He'd have done just six weeks basic training and then resumed his career as the world's most successful and popular singer, entertainer, and movie star. But here's the thing. Being in Special Services meant he would have to perform a minimum of four concerts a year. Maybe more but at least four. For Free. They would film each performance and then sell them to TV stations all around the world, with every single dollar going to the armed forces. And the more popular he becomes the more money he will generate for Uncle Sam. Sending him off to be an ordinary GI Joe, in Germany or wherever, is the financial equivalent of the Wall Street Crash for the armed forces.

The generals say they would like to run some figures by them. How many countries around the world would pay top dollar to show an Elvis concert? Let's say 100, but it's probably an underestimate. The sales of each show would bring in at least $25 million, including advertising and sponsorship; four shows a year over the two years of his draft equals $200 million. Do the President and his advisers know how many tanks, ships, and jet fighters $200 million would buy?

Nixon, who now looks so damp he could be sitting in a sauna, is worried that 'losing' that amount of money might be an impeachable offence. Not good for the President or him. He mops his face with a handkerchief and asks what can be done.

For now, the generals tell him, leave it to us. They have a meeting coming up with Elvis's manager, Colonel Parker, and they will explain that there has been a snafu in the system, something he will surely understand as an ex-military man. They will assure him that Elvis will be reassigned to Special Services.

Colonel Parker thinks it might make a difference and score a few bonus points if he turns up for the meeting at the Pentagon wearing his full dress uniform of a Colonel in the Virginia Fencibles. It doesn't. But sporting so many medals and so much gold braid means he would have been perfect in a Gilbert & Sullivan comic opera. There are a lot of smiles from the top brass as he walks in, so he assumes they are pleased to see him.

However, the atmosphere quickly turns frosty, as he reports later to Elvis and the family at Graceland.

"So what went wrong?" asks Elvis.

"When I heard what they're proposing – pretty well everything." His body wobbles with indignation like an enormous Hawaiian-shirted jelly.

Right away at the start of the meeting, it is agreed that Elvis should be reassigned to Special Services, do six weeks' basic training and then resume his career. Mission accomplished, he thinks, but as he is about to leave they ask him to sit down again.

For a moment he thinks they are going to ask him about the Oval Office ashtray that he was surreptitiously going to take with him, but no.

"And here comes the iniquity, the injustice, the scandal..." His vocabulary soon expires, and he puffs furiously on his Walmart cigar while he attempts to regain his train of thought.

"In return for being in Special Services, Elvis has to do a minimum of four shows a year which the army will film and then sell to TV stations around the world," he splutters and fizzes like a firework about to explode. "They will make hundreds of millions of dollars. But listen to this: not one cent goes to Elvis! The armed forces pocket the lot! Those army boys make Al Capone look like somebody running a kiddies nursery. What they are doing ought to be a court-martial offence."

"That's terrible," sighs Elvis, shaking his head, and seeks consolation by helping himself to a couple of Hershey bars from a plate. "But what can we do?"

"I'm saying this is robbery carried out with a draft notice instead of a gun. And we've gotta take a stand against it," declares the Colonel.

"We??!!"

"Yes, Elvis. We cannot let them get away with stealing all this money. The way we stop this larceny is for you to join the army as an ordinary GI. Just be a good soldier and serve out your time. But do no shows and give no interviews. That'll teach 'em a lesson."

"But what about my career, my family," wails Elvis. "I'm going to be stuck in the armed forces for two years. I'll be lonely, I'll have no friends and no future."

Colonel Parker does not mention, because it is no longer part of his plan, that the navy offers to set up a special company made up of Elvis's closest friends and other men from Memphis, and as part of the deal, he can perform in Las Vegas and have his own private quarters. The army's bid includes sending him around the world, visiting army bases. All any of the armed forces want is for him to join Special Services and perform at least four shows a year. That is all. But the Colonel has no intention of letting them walk away with upwards of $200 million.

He says, "We've got to come up with a plan, and we will. And remember, Elvis, I'll be there, marching alongside you every step of the way."

"Will my boy still be with that nice Sergeant Bilko and be on TV where we can see him?" asks his mother.

Elvis shakes his head almost imperceptibly; the Colonel notes this and asserts that they will move heaven and earth to get him to Fort Baxter.

The plan that they come up with will see Elvis complete the 'King Creole' movie and spend a couple of weeks at the RCA studios in Nashville making a stockpile of records such as 'One Night' and 'A Fool Such As I' that can be released from time to time to keep him in the charts and in the minds of his fans. The producer, Hal Wallis, has promised to have a movie ready to start shooting about his life in the army the moment he sets foot back in the United States.

Elvis laughs bitterly, "Will it be a comedy?"

"If I had my way it would be like one of those 1930s Jimmy Cagney gangster movies," declares Colonel Parker. "And a lot of generals would get shot in the course of being robbed."

Rock and roll will be a here today gone tomorrow fad, he reasons to himself, and these two years in the army will allow the middle-class furore about Elvis to die down, and for him to come back with his career moving in a slightly different direction.

But Elvis is unhappy about this, complaining that he does not want to be turned into some sort of dude dressed up in a tuxedo and bow tie, doing the cabaret circuit and singing the same dreary standards as everybody else.

He tells his manager, "You know, I think I'd die if the first thing I do after leaving the army and coming back to the USA, is to appear in a TV show with some old crooner all dressed up like I'm going out to dinner. Man, that's so square. That's not what I am and it's not who my fans want me to be," he adds with feeling. "I want to stay true to my roots."

His manager explains that in the long term he will have to mature and develop as an artiste; he can't always be a hillybilly rocker. Think maybe more Johnny Ray in future and less Jerry Lee Lewis is how he puts it. But he promises, crossing his fingers behind his back, that the evolution will be gradual and not an overnight thing.

In the meantime, unbeknown to Elvis, he is busy organising some new merchandise material for the fans to buy to reflect Elvis being in the army. He has already placed an order for several tons of surplus army uniforms, having agreed on a price of $5 dollars a ton. This 'criminal' price he has to pay is another grudge with the military. He has primed his network of sweatshops in Bangladesh and Soweto to work on projects such as removing the 'I Love Elvis' logos from old stocks of fringed cowboy hats and sticking them on army camouflage caps. There will be camouflage cushions made from the old uniforms with slogans such as 'I'm serving with Elvis', 'I Love Elvis' dog tags, and army-style tin coffee mugs. The result of Colonel Parker's background of years in carny and working on stalls selling gimcrack gifts, before becoming the manager of singers like Eddy Arnold, Hank Snow, and Elvis, means that he is an expert in being able to mine the depths of tackiness deeper than anyone else. And Elvis joining the army promises to be a motherlode in merchandise for him to exploit.

He has even commissioned a number of novelty items like plastic army hand grenades: you pull the pin, wait 10 seconds, squeeze the grenade, and a spray of a chokingly sweet, chemically made perfume is released. Two-year calendars so that fans can cross out the days till Elvis returns, and 'Eat like Elvis' army chow TV dinners are also being developed.

Elvis calls a meeting of the family to tell them the news that he will be posted to Fort Hood in Texas.

Immediately tears start in the eyes of his mother and trickle down her cheeks. She protests that she has set her heart on him going to Fort Baxter to be with that nice Sergeant Bilko, to work in the motorpool and have lots of fun with Private Doberman and the other guys in the platoon. "And seeing you on TV will make me rest easy, Elvis," she pleads.

Vernon shouts out, "Son, you've been double-crossed. The army should hang its head in shame. Let's get the Colonel on this right away."

"Hey, Mom, Dad, Texas ain't so far from Roseville in Kansas, where Sergeant Bilko is based. And anyway, that's the bad news."

"You mean there's some good news comin' out of all this?" asks Vernon.

Despite everything that has gone on, the army has been very good to him, explains Elvis. Strictly speaking, as a GI, he should live on the post at Fort Hood. But they've waived the rules and said he can live in his own house off the post. And his Mom and Dad and grandmother Minnie Mae can live there with him. Now there is a different kind of tears and whoops of delight as all four of them clasp each other in a big family hug.

Minnie Mae is getting excited. "Mebbe Fort Hood is named after Granpappy Hood, an' mebbe there's some of our kinfolk a-livin' around there," she shouts. "Hee Har. It's party time. Ah'm a-gonna git that jug o' moonshine ah've bin a-keepin' fer a special occasion, an' ah got me some chitlins ah can fry up. We're a-gonna have us an ole style Tupelo jug-an'-jig."

"It will be like a big family holiday," Elvis tells them. "OK, it won't be Graceland but it will be our home from home and we'll be together."

It is the first time he has seen his mother smile for weeks. Although Elvis can't yet bring himself to tell his parents that at some point in the future he may well be sent to Germany, he reminds Colonel Parker of his promise to be there with him 'every step of the way'.

142

"Of course," declares his manager, straining to be as jovial as possible. "Mrs. Parker has already packed my lederhosen."

He continues, "The worst thing that can happen is that I may have to follow you over there just a little bit later than planned. Naturally, I want to be there as soon as possible, you understand. But there are a few contracts that need to be signed off, and there seems to be some sort of issue with my passport. But don't worry, I'm sure everything will be fine. Germany, here I come."

Notes

- The health of Elvis's mother Gladys deteriorated while the family was staying with him at Fort Hood. She and Vernon returned to Memphis to see her personal physician; she was transferred to hospital and died on August 14, 1958, aged 46.
- There was never any prospect of Colonel Parker going to Germany. In fact, he never left the United States during his lifetime. He entered the country illegally as a young man and he was always worried that he may not be issued with a passport or, even worse, could be deported.
- Elvis's first TV appearance soon after leaving the army was the Frank Sinatra Show. Besides Elvis's new single 'Stuck On You', the show featured a duet with Elvis singing Sinatra's hit 'Witchcraft' and Sinatra performing 'Love Me Tender'. Elvis wore a tuxedo and a bow tie.
- Series 2 of the Sgt Bilko TV series showed an episode in which a rock and roll singer called Elvin Pelvin is drafted into the army and sent to Fort Baxter. It was aired in March 1957.

Ends

Robert Wells became an Elvis fan at the age of 11
and he remains one more than 60 years later. This
deep affection and knowledge translate into these
stories which present a comic vision of the life of the
King of Rock and Roll.

He has made a pilgrimage to Graceland, Tupelo and
the Sun recording studio, as well as spending a night
in the Burning Love suite at Heartbreak Hotel.

He is a former journalist whose first job was with the
Wolverhampton Express & Star, and later a corporate
communications publisher based in London. A
widower with a son and daughter, he and his partner
live in Leighton Buzzard.

Robert's interests include, naturally, rock and roll,
and he has amassed a superb collection of Elvis
records, his favourite being 'Lawdy Miss Clawdy'.
Other interests are Charles Dickens, ancient Greek
and Roman history, and gravestones.

The publisher

*He who stops
getting better
stops being good.*

This is the motto of novum publishing, and our focus
is on finding new manuscripts, publishing them and
offering long-term support to the authors.
Our publishing house was founded in 1997, and since
then it has become THE expert for new authors and
has won numerous awards.

**Our editorial team will peruse each manuscript
within a few weeks free of charge and without
obligation.**

You will find more information about
novum publishing and our books on the internet:

www.novum-publishing.co.uk